UNFAMILIAR SHORES

ALSO BY PETER M. BALL

Short Story Collections

The Birdcage Heart & Other Strange Tales

Not Quite The End Of The World Just Yet: Short Stories & Strange Futures

These Strange & Magic Things: Short Stories

The Gold Coast Ragnarök Trilogy

Exile

Frost

Crusade

Gold Coast Ragnarok (Omnibus)

Dana Valkyrie Adventures

White Harbour War

The Miriam Aster Case Files

Horn

Bleed

Unicorns, Fey, and a Hardboiled Dame (Omnibus)

UNFAMILIAR SHORES

SHORT STORIES

PETER M. BALL

GenrePunk Books (an imprint of Brain Jar Press)
PO Box 6687
Upper Mt Gravatt, QLD, 4122
Australia
GenrePunk Books: www.PeterMBall.com
Brain Jar Press: www.BrainJarPress.com

All stories Copyright © 2024 by Peter M. Ball. Early chapters of this book were previously published on the authors Patreon and Eclectic Projects magazine, sometimes in very different forms

The moral right of Peter M. Ball to be identified as the author of this work has been asserted.

All rights reserved. No part of this book may be reproduced in any form or by any electronic or mechanical means, including information storage and retrieval systems, without written permission from the author, except for the use of brief quotations in a book review.

Cover design by Brain Jar Press
Cover Image: night scenery of the big lighthouse in futuristic world, Tithi Luadthong/Shutterstock

ISBN: 978-1-922479-94-5 (paperback) | 978-1-922479-95-2 (Ebook)

CONTENTS

The Cars 1
Put Not Your Faith In Hope 11
Four Mohocks, Sent Abroad 15
Median Survival Time 19
Warm Milk & Whiskey 27
The Fucking-Shitfull-Goddamned-Asshole-
Noodlecocked-Motherfucker Has To Die 31
This Is How You Step Up 35
The Fighter 44
It's Not A Job 49
Nos, The Beetle Slayer 58
Infection Vectors 64
On The Corner of Caxton and Petrie, 12:04 AM 72
A Good Theif's Choices 77
The Chap Who Wanted to Be Commander Flag 83
One Last Job, And Then Sleep 89
The Deal 98
I'm Afraid Of The Big Bad Wolf 107
Or For Eternity Hold Your Piece 118
Six Cats Go Camping 125
The Final Season 143

Story Notes 177
Acknowledgments 185

THE CARS

1.

My friend Tess fought an Escalade in the early days of the uprising. Given the lack of weapons and customised tools in those early days, her survival earns her the title of "bravest woman I've ever met."

The midnight-black SUV tailed her down Warwick Avenue, prowling between the streetlights like an oversized jungle cat. Tess believed there to be a driver who meant her harm, responded with instincts honed by self-defense classes and a lifetime of scanning the world around her for potential threats. She kept herself visible and made a beeline for the Halcyon Street intersection, hoping to find safety amid the crowd.

These were sensible choices given the rules of the world as we knew it, but Tess quickly learned those rules were changing. The Escalade fired its engine and followed her into Halcyon Street, carving a path through the foot traffic. Tess freaked and clambered upwards, scaling the concrete newsstand on the far side of the intersection.

The Escalade rammed the structure, bumper crumpling under the impact, and Tess had the nous to hold on. The car attempted to dislodge her three more times, damaging its motor, and only then did Tess climb down.

She knew the owner of the newsstand kept a baseball bat under the register. He'd threatened a couple of young thieves with it, when Tess first arrived in the neighbourhood. She laid claim to the weapon and fought back.

Witnesses claim Tess wailed on the Escalade for five straight minutes, smashing windows, denting doors. Still believing she'd find a predator inside, someone to beat on and hold accountable when the police arrived.

By the time she realized there was no driver, Tess had a different plan in mind. One that didn't rely on brute force.

2.

I could say I preferred it when cars were inanimate. Immobile objects without keys in the ignition and a foot on the accelerator. Easily trapped in place by a park brake or the careful siphoning of a fuel tank. They moved with caution back then, slaking their thirst for blood intermittently, content to winnow our numbers with the slow application of carbon dioxide and the occasional hit-and-run.

I could claim I miss the good old days when we pretended —by mutual agreement—that sidewalks were safe places to walk. Only a madman bore down on pedestrians, leaping the gutter to squish our delicate bodies beneath the snarling weight of a fast-moving chassis.

I could profess a desire to return to those days, to the version of myself who worked in an office and ordered home delivery three nights a week. The version of myself who drove cars without thinking, believing they were tame. Like you, I daydream of escaping to Denmark, or Sweden, or Bangladesh, countries where the widespread embrace of bikes—motorized and pedal powered—diminished the impact of the cars shucking their disguise and laying claim to the streets.

I could tell these lies, and they would be comforting. So many of us hate the new world, the sheer challenge of survival. So many of us believe things were better when we didn't have a common enemy.

3.

Lacey pissed off the High Chief of the local Chevrolet clan, and our holdout became targets by association. We realized the scale of the problem last Thursday, when a sky-blue '76 Malibu leapt out of an alleyway and mauled Theo just two blocks from our squat. The older cars are vicious pricks, still angry about the years spent hiding in plain sight, restraining their baser impulses in the name of a long-term plan.

The attack broke sixteen bones in Theo, would have killed him if I hadn't been there to haul him into a nearby townhouse and up to the second floor. I spent the next hour playing cat-and-mouse, laying road spikes and luring the chevy into them, taking pot-shots at the ancient Chevy's tires. The old bastard was canny, knew all the tricks. Not so reckless as some of the younger cars, fresh off the assembly line. Smart enough to charge through a wall and surprise me while I felt safe.

In a lifetime of close calls with cars, he came the closest to taking me out.

But I got him in the end, and I hauled Theo's broken ass back to the squat where the doc could check him out. We all gathered, and I laid out what happened, talked through how it would change things for a while.

That's when Lacey raised her hand and confessed it might be her fault.

4.

The cars rarely hunt alone these days, although they proved to be territorial and tribal once freed from the great façade. There are sixteen great tribes in our city, nominally controlled by the Audis, who lay claim to the highways and arterial roads. Our squat—like many surviving patches of humanity—sticks to the upper levels of buildings because cars cannot climb stairs. We fortify roads with spikes and ditches, makeshift landmines, armed guards. We band together for mutual survival, surviving on scavenged foods and rooftop gardens, jury-rigged generators and a careful network of information shared with the other outposts of survivors like ours.

The cars nest in underground parking lots, prowl the streets in search of prey.

There are worst things than being hunted by the Chevys. Their numbers are small, compared to the Fords and the Holdens. The Hondas, the BMWs and the Volvos who claim the beachside suburbs where humans once holidayed. When debate breaks out in our small squat, arguing about how we should handle Lacey's breach of trust and the anger of the Chevrolet, there is some discussion about going to war. A general belief we can take the Chevys out, given the size of their tribe.

We've heard variations of this argument before, always spawned of a common belief: Cars do not replicate themselves. Humans designed and built them, their numbers born off assembly lines rather than procreation. Yes, they have the advantage of prodigious, terrifying numbers, but those numbers don't replenish.

Vocal advocates for war argue the lack of baby cars is an opportunity. Thin the herds, and we can out-breed them.

These passionate, glorious fools fail to consider two things. First, our own depleted numbers, however fecund we are as a species, create a significant obstacle.

Second, the first car appeared in 1886; we considered them docile, inanimate things for one-hundred and thirty-eight years. Any predator species capable of such restraint, for such a period, has a plan to replenish their numbers in the event humanity fights back. They have, after all, sidestepped our assumptions they'd fade away once the fuel ran out.

There are those who argue for war, but I believe otherwise. Better to placate and avoid, playing to our strengths.

5.

My friend Tess defeated the damaged Escalade by luring it towards the river, provoking a charge and deftly avoiding the attack, letting momentum carry the black SUV through the guardrail and into the water. Tires spun as it fought to free itself and the petrochemical stink of its death lingered long after the police, the paramedics, and the firefighters arrived. They treated the wounded and the dying, cleaned up the parts of Halcyon Street damaged by the Escalade's murderous rampage.

Two officers questioned Tess, hoping for answers. Her claims nobody sat behind the wheel were met with disbelief, even after a team of divers searched for a body. Three police divers went down, and only two returned. They could find no sign of the Escalade, nor their missing partner.

I share this story with the war enthusiasts in our squat. They fail to learn the lesson; argue we can use the river to defeat the Chevys and lay claim to more of the city we once called home.

We vote, as a collective. The collective choice is not a good one.

6.

A smarter man would abandon the squat before they antagonized a tribe of Chevys, but there's more to life than pure survival. These people are my friends, wrong-headed choices or otherwise, and I want to stand beside them for as long as I can stomach it. And so I take part in the early planning, figuring where we'll lay our road spikes and where to place mines. I walk Lacey through the plan, the ways she'll serve as bait for the Chevys and lure them into the trap. I make it clear the decision is hers—vote or no, we can't force her to do this—and Lacey admits she got us into this and feels responsible for getting us out.

We arm the healthy—guns, long spears for bursting tires, and blunt weapons for the up-close fighting. We drill the moves, practice scattering and getting off the ground. Convince ourselves we know how to fight a car and avoid the counterattack.

The mood in the squat grows buoyant, as though we have a chance.

In this, as ever, we're optimistic fools, but that's always defined humanity's relationship with cars. Even in the days we thought them simple, we overestimated the danger they represented and our ability to survive when things went wrong. How else do you explain our reluctance to switch away from fuels? Our insistence on driving SUVs, despite their lethality to pedestrians?

How else does the simple act of strapping yourself into a car and driving at a hundred miles an hour make any kind of sense?

7.

We're all nervous. We finished breakfast in terse silence, the strongest of us drifting off in dribs and drabs to prepare for the fight to come. We washed dishes in communal tubs, shoulder to shoulder in the small kitchen, eager to leave our mundane jobs completed should the worst occur. I found my way to the northern balcony and watch the sun rise over the city. The rumble of engines is everywhere, an omnipresent background noise we pretend not to notice.

Lacey drifts out to the far side of the balcony. Neither of us says much, not with the impending fight. Nobody wants their last words to be something stupid. Lacey puts both hands on the balcony rail. She's a slight woman, verging on gaunt these days when food is harder to come by. There's scar tissue on her right shoulder, legacy of an early encounter with a Commodore that ended poorly. Theo and I saved her from that encounter, dragged her back and watched her heal and stoked her hatred for the cars. Another soldier we could use to keep the squat safe, or so we thought at the time.

To my shame, I ponder knocking her out. Taking her out and leaving her for the Chevys, placating the chieftain instead of going to war. The raw survival math makes it a sensible choice. No need for people to risk their lives, to burn through our limited resources.

"I can hear you thinking, Deacon Whitley," Lacey says. "And I don't want this any more than you do."

I know the regrets that sink in before a battle, the propensity for rash decisions. I've brought trouble down on the squat before, had to rely on them to save my ass. I've fought for good plans the collective voted down.

I would like the chance to experience that regret again, but this time I fear the collective has made a catastrophic choice.

8.

Lacey hits the streets, feigning a covert scramble from squat to the safety of the Salmat Building two blocks down. The rest of us keep to the sky ways—the ropes strung between buildings and makeshift bridges—taking the slowest route to the ambush site down by the river. Everything falls apart if the Chevrolets sense our purpose and our numbers; we need them angry, focused on Lacey's made scramble to escape, not watching for attacks on their flanks or newly blocked streets that push them towards the water.

We lost sight of Lacey during the first hour. No choice but to trust she could evade the Chevys and make it to us, line them up for the push into the water. We crept up on the ambush site and hunkered down to wait. Down on the streets, on the far side of the block, we could hear the rumble of engines and the squeak of tires on the blacktop.

I'm one of the team on Smith Street, watching over the newly installed mine field on one of the Chevrolet's principal thoroughfares. There's four of us, spears in hand, breath caught in our throat. Waiting for the signal the ambush is a go. Somebody—at first, I think it's Theo, but he's still in the infirmary waiting for his bones to fuse—makes a joke about the long wait.

It's not a good joke, but we laugh, then stifle our voices lest we're overheard and the entire plans for naught.

Minutes turned into an hour. One hour turned into three. I log all the ways this plan can go wrong, how many of them are still likely this far into the wait.

We holed up on the second floor of an old hardware store,

its shelves long-since picked clean. Nothing left now by debris and smashed windows and a ground floor trashed by passing cars pursuing humans too dumb to go up. As the wait heads into its fourth hour, we take turns going to the back of the store and warming up, twisting fatigue out of muscles unused to staying immobile for this long.

A comrade touches my shoulder, signals it's my turn to go stretch. I wave him down the line, unwilling to miss the car's arrival. I want to be here when Lacey tears down Smith Street, weaving between the buildings, hunted by a flotilla of cars eager for her blood.

Of course, it's a terrible plan. Lacey could be dead by now. Or penned in by circling Chevrolets, unable to make a break for the ambush site. Cars don't fatigue like humans do, and they need less fuel these days.

I voice the question—"When do we call it?"—and nobody answers. We settle in for another hour, ears cocked to the sound of engines

Five hours. Six. It has to be over. I figure we should all go home, but I don't want to say it out loud. I don't want to die out here, today. I don't want to be broken on the streets, crushed beneath a tire or battered against the wall by a bloodstained bumper.

9.

Our spotter signals: Lacey's on her way. We grab our spears and form up. Lacey sprints down the Smith Street sidewalk, breaking out of the front door of the old supermarket, dancing between the mine placements like they're not even there.

The Chevrolets pursue in numbers, fourteen cars roaring down Smith Street as Lacey darts through a smashed display window in the Halstead Mall.

There's an art to placing land mines, especially the make-shift armaments we've tinkered together in the squat. Theo trained our people well, and as the fourteen Chevys roll down Smith we hold our breath and hope they'll do the job.

The Chevys spread across the street, moving to circle the mall. The first explosion rips through the engine of the 2015 Suburban leading the way, and three more detonate in short order as the rest of the pack veers away from the fire.

It's as good an opening as we'll get, so our squad readies spears and clears the windows, charging in to puncture tires and fade away before the cars can react. The first stage in a plan, harrying the Chevrolets to the point where they stop thinking and focus on the hunt.

To my surprise, it all goes smoothly. In the space of twelve minutes, we disable six Chevrolets. Two are destroyed entirely. Our squad fades into the nearby buildings, heading for the top floor, and only Perkins and Maxwell are missing when we stop and do a headcount.

On the street, the roar of engines. The burn of rubber on the blacktop.

The Chevrolet are angry and eager to taste blood, and phase one of the plan is successful. It feels like a victory in the moment, but I'm all too aware it cannot.

Fourteen Chevys are a small fraction of their numbers, and none of them were the chief of the tribe.

Damaging cars is satisfying, but it's a spit in the ocean compared to the larger problem, and our plan relies too much on luck and whittling their numbers down.

Still, my part is done. My obligation to the squat discharged.

I gather my spear and head to higher ground, uninterested in a long farewell or opportunities for some eager squatter to try and change my mind.

10.

I wandered the city for three weeks, searching for an alternate squat to join. Used the second floor of an abandoned Burrito Hut as a temporary base, unearthing tins of beans and corn from their yet-to-be-plundered stores.

I don't know if the plan succeeded, if Laccy and my former

squat mates survived their altercation, but there are still Chevrolet on the roads and the other tribes are out in force now. Mammoth haul trucks migrated from the mining cities up north, hauling their seventy-ton frames through streets designed for hatchbacks and economical sedans.

Something has changed. We can all feel it. The cars have realized humanity is still a threat, inventive enough to take down larger, stronger predators encased in a shell of steel. By the time I join a new squat on Blackman Road, the rumbles have already started: "If we winnow their numbers, we might just have a chance. If we take out the high chief of the Holdens, there may be a window where we can do more."

As if the problem is taking out one car, or a dozen, or even a whole damn city. As if there weren't over a billion more of the fuckers out there, hungry for blood and flesh, and eager to run us down.

I don't tell them the story of Tess this time. There are already rumors about the squat who fought, about Lacey's sacrifice to the cause. Rumors suggesting my former squat succeeded, taking out the chief of the Chevrolet and the rest of the damn tribe.

The new squat cleaves to these rumors, refusing to look at the obvious. If they succeeded, why aren't they here gathering recruits? If the fight was so successful, why not escalate to a full-fledged war? I knew these people and their plans. Their dream of living free once more, walking streets without the fear of being hit from behind by a charging vehicle.

But I the new guy, and nobody wants to hear I walked away from their new source of hope. It takes time and respect to mount a response anyone will hear. Time, respect, and the trust of the squat.

I fear I do not have the time to gain these things before it's time to move on and search for a new home again.

PUT NOT YOUR FAITH
IN HOPE

"It's claimed we fled into the God's Eye to escape the end of the world." Doctor Levinson rests a foot against the lowest rung of the scaffold. "If true, one has to wonder if this was intended as a permeant solution, or a temporary home."

"Does it matter?"

He smiles at me. "Perhaps. Rumor has it the gods created the world, Just as they triggered its final days. Intent could tell us much about the world that was."

He's a handsome man, square-jawed and blue-eyed, blessed with rangy strength. Determined to be the final Optomeister, the one who coaxes the great eyelid open and sends us back into the world abandoned for our place in the God's Eye.

Levinson ascends the scaffold with a practiced surety, re-checking the networked cogs, electrodes, and pulleys built against the Eye's interior surface. He senses my gaze and pauses, rubs a leather-gloved hand across his forehead.

I'm not mean to like him, but I do. Levinson's left cheek dimples when he smiles. Blonde hair hangs loose around his angular face, cheeks flushed with excitement. Shame touches my neck and I feign interest in the checklist.

"Soon," Levinson calls. "Soon we'll see the world beyond. It's a great day, Mister Pekins." His feet clatter along the gangplank as Levinson heads for junction T4-K12. One of the countless labeled components which make up the great machine.

The ground-level checklist logs twenty-seven tasks, divided and grouped into eight categories. I start at the top—generator —and feign interest in following the designated checks. Up top, on the fourth scaffold layer, Levinson whistles as he works. The sheer exuberance of the man galls me, given what I'm tasked to do. I had not expected to *care* so much, nor share the thrum of excitement as Levinson *speculates*, pondering the world beyond or how the Eye works.

"Cog T4-L23 is loose," Levinson calls. "I'll tighten her up and start on the next row."

Kicking the generator is not on my checklist, but I give into the impulse. My toe crunches against the archaic metal chassis —a precious relic from the days before the Eye—and I bite down on a curse.

Levinson's footsteps clatter against the gangplanks, pause another level up. "T5-A12 is wonky too. The apprentices were careless on this stretch."

They were not. Levinson hand-picked our apprentices himself, his selections diligent and exacting as any other component of his grand ambition to use the machine to winch the God's Eye open. They would sooner die than leave shoddy work, disappointing him.

I know, because more than a few have expired in the last few hours.

"Perhaps we should pause the test?" My voice doesn't crack, posing the question. I feared it would. "Strip and rebuild, to be sure?"

"I think we'll spot the errors. A well-crafted checklist is powerful, Mister Perkins."

They are. It's half the problem. For sixteen generations there have been Optomeisters, hand-selected for their intelligence and complete lack of practical skills. How Levinson eluded the systems designed to block the *competent* from the role is beyond me. He tightens the bolts on T5-A12 and moves on, whistling. Takes the ladder to the next level.

I know my duty, although I don't want to do it. For a moment I crouch behind the generator and pray to the slumbering god that now is the time to wake and remove the decisions from my hands.

The heavy lid draped over the Eye remains closed, swirling phosphenes marring the dark. I did not know the term, once. Levinson's earliest experiments stimulated patches of the Eye with an electrical current, observing the impact lights on the back of the eyelid. For a year, he mapped the more constant dots and circles, theorized external pressure caused the burning red ring in the top right corner. "The God still lives, Perkins," he said. "We don't need to open the eyelid ourselves, just coax the muscles around the Eye into doing what comes naturally."

Levinson invested sixteen years in building the machine, which turns theory into practice. His glorious, orderly mind repaired every sabotage attempt I've instigated. My father—who guarded the Eye before more me, just his grandfather stood guard over the Optomeisters of their era—explained the situation and let duty guide my steps.

I abandon my boots and pad barefoot to the ladder, follow Levinson's voice. Up seven floors, the weight of the heavy knife strapped to my chest pulling at my balance. My breath is harsh, and bile itches the back of my throat.

My father said God's Eye needs the hope we'll see the world beyond one day, but hope is so different from success. Hope is forever a bright beacon that shines in the darkness, while success is a chance for something grubby and broken, a ravaged world ruled by the nightmares which forced us to abscond to the safety of the Eye.

"How do we know?" I asked my father. "What makes you so sure we're right and Levinson is wrong?"

My father deigned not to answer a question so obvious. Perhaps the world has changed in the long century since our retreat. Perhaps we're missing a paradise out there, on the far side of the dark, heavy lid. And perhaps things had gotten worse, in the long centuries we'd spent in God's Eye protective shell.

"Place not your faith in hope," he said. "Trust in what is known."

I find Levinson on T7, preparing to clamber up top. He turns towards me, smiles, giddy now so many decades of study and plans might culminate in the long-held dream. He believes me a partner, an ally.

I keep the knife low and tight against my side. He doesn't spot the weapon until I'm close.

Levinson's a smart man. Puts it together fast. What the blade means, what I've done to him. "No," he says, desperate. Raises both hands. "Perkins, please. No."

I must.

I bring the knife up. "It's easier if you close your eyes."

But Levinson's blue eyes stare at me until I push the knife in.

FOUR MOHOCKS, SENT ABROAD

Ain't like I planned a trip to Faerie, but me Da figured it was this or the gallows. Not entirely wrongly, given her majesty offered one hundred pounds a head for any Mohock captured and delivered to the coppers. Da figured me for a dunce who'd get stubbed by some fortune seeker eager for a little scratch, an' he cut some deals and wily trades to ensure me and a bunch of my fellow rowdies got sent away for a stretch. It was supposed to be a four-week spell in Glastonbury, where me uncle has himself a house, but somehow we got ourselves waylaid and found ourselves somewhere very else indeed.

An' as the Queen of the Winter Court told us, when we first arrived, Faerie does not give up what it's claimed without putting up a fight.

"Right by us," we fazzled her. "Ain't a Mohock alive who's afraid of a scrap, nor one who comes out the worst for wear of it. We've rousted the London Watch enough, and rolled her best and brightest down Snow Hill in a barrel."

That seemed to amuse the Winter Queen, 'cause her pale lip curled up a little, and Jack Nonce got into himself to go a-boasting about how dangerous the four of us were. He told tales about tipping the lion and tumbling women-folk on their legs, and gathering around some poor barmy schoolboy and sweatering him with sword points to the buttocks until he was rightly pinked. All in good fun, back home, but it felt weak and foolish here, standing in the frost-rimed courtyard of the Queen surrounded by fey and deadly beasties, each wild, cruel, and beautiful as the point of a well-forged knife.

"Anything you want of us," Nonce said. "Any act of violence we can do, or service we may perform, say the word and we four will get it scuppered, quick-smartish, and buy our way home to our friends and luvvies."

The entire court laughed at that one, and I got myself a funny feeling, but the Queen curled her lip a little more and agreed to offer us a mission. Something suited to our talents, four dangerous men such as we.

All we had to do was deliver a message to her sister on the far side of Faerie, and get it done before the seasons changed, lest we found ourselves negotiating anew with the Summer Queen, who held sway once the sun shone and the snows melted.

"No problem," says Jack Nonce, even as the rest of us hemmed and hawed about those claims, but the Queen made it clear we ain't got no other choice, and ain't nobody going to cross her and offer us aid she won't, which is how we all ended up on the road with naught but our swords and knives and straight razors, finding our way across the strange landscape with knots of hope and desperation tangled up in our squicky insides.

Things went wrong immediate-like, on account of us not knowing the ins and outs of Faerie, and it seems a right shame that Jack Nonce wasn't the first to run foul of the fey folk. Instead, that honor fell to Big Eared Roger, who got the notion to hassle this old man on the road who turned out to be anything but.

"Aye, lads," Big Ear said upon spotting the wizened figure. "Here's a bit of fun, like, and a chance to earn some local dosh besides?"

I tried to talk him out of out it, but we'd been in Faerie a while now, and all of us were feeling hungry on account of Dunstan Timbs warnings not to eat nothing offered as a gift or courtesy. Big Ear had a belly to match his flappers, and a ready sword at the best of times, so he trotted off to growl and menace and sticky-sticky with his blade.

Whereupon he learned that not all in Faerie is exactly what it seems, and the old man warbled into some kind of giant and snatched Big Ear in one might hand, flinging him at an ice-sheathed river where Big Ear promptly cracked his noggin and bled himself to death.

When that titanic, elderly monster asked if any of us wanted the same, we assured him Big Ear was acting alone, and begged off any further rumblings.

We four had become three in an instant, and it weren't like that was the end.

Dunstan Timbs knew more about Faerie than most, on account of his nan being all wily to the old ways, and he wracked his memory to keep us out of trouble for the next few days. We worked a day tilling a troll field to earn a little dosh and used that to buy ourselves a meal of bread and fruits and hunks of meat whose providence we neither asked about nor truly wanted to know.

But Dunstan Timbs had a weakness, like all man do, and when the road passed through some lonely fens that never froze with the break of winter, he heard a song out in the muck and caught himself a glimpse of a raven-haired beauty who beckoned for him to come closer. Me and Jack Nonce didn't hear naught, and we figured it for some trick, but after two days of talking Dunstan out of wading into the water, we lost him when Jack Nonce fell asleep when he was supposed to be keeping watch.

And so it became me and Jack Nonce, a pair of men traveling alone, and I weren't none too happy that he was the man I got stuck with. I blamed him right hard for starting all this, and getting Dunstan and Big Ears scuppered, and he reminded me we wouldn't be in Faerie at all if my Da hadn't panicked and sent us away, on account of Old Annie's bounty. Which is, as you say, fair enough a point, but half the reason her Majesty put a price on our head was the hijinks Jack Nonce urged for, time and again. Never was one for egging boys on like Jack, always looking for another fight, another victim, another excess that might terrify the passing gentry.

After a day of going back and forth, we lapsed into silent drudgery. Walking step-by-step together, saying naught and exchanging no acknowledgment of the other except the occasional shove or baleful side-eye.

Then we made camp on a lonely hill, near a snow-covered barrow with black stones around its entryway, and by then neither of us were stupid enough to suggest going inside to get out of the cold.

Or, at least, I thought that were true, but I woke to find Jack Nonce was gone, and there's one set of footprints coming out of that horrible blackness and two pairs returning afterwards. Everything Nonce owned had vanished with him, except for a blood splattered razor, and I ain't entirely sure if those stains were his blood or whatever took 'im.

An', truth be told, I miss my Da, and the thought of being bountied don't seem so bad no more. Any punishment Old Queen Anne dished out was going to be faster and cleaner than this, wandering through a strange land all alone, with your best buds dead and gone.

Surely, the troubles we caused weren't worth ending up like this.

I want to go home right sore and true, but Faerie don't give up nobody without a fight, an' I'm the last of us left to barney with it.

Which means I should press on, like, and deliver this message to the Queen of Summer.

All I've got to do is play it smart, like. Not fall for any of the malarky that cost me Nonce and Big Ears and Dunstan Timbs.

All I've got to do is forget what it means to be a Mohock, because this place will rumble mortal folk far sneakier and far worse than anything we did up on Snow Hill, and it ain't like I was the brightest spark in our lot, not by a long shot

MEDIAN SURVIVAL TIME

They sat in the bubble port at the far end of Corridor B-13, at the table up against the observation window that looked over the surface. The terrain on the other side of the borosilicate glass was dark, jagged rock and plumes of crimson dust lit by the bloody light smeared against the horizon. The colors of sunset reminded Holst of Ganymede, the missile and the fire and long minutes pinned against her seat. Her unit screaming, dying, dead. The vanishing agony as flame-seared nerves in her arm, leg, and face died and felt no more.

On this side of the glass there was oxygen and clustered seating, the warmth that came with too many bodies crammed together and left to sweat. They said you barely noticed the smell after your first week on planet, but a year and eleven months have proved that incorrect. Holst and the man she knew as Breech were imports, hired guns on a three-year contract. Not that there were many guns on the colony, or much call to use them for enforcement in this part of space. Breech concealed a knife for any dirty work he came across. Holst didn't even bother with that.

People stared at Holst and they noticed Breech as an afterthought. Even here, where wounds were left to heal naturally, her scars were noticed and remembered.

Two hundred meters down B-13 was the first airlock, the

chamber beyond little more than a place to strap into a suit before you stepped onto the surface. A hundred meters further, an intersection that led into the complex carved into the mountain.

Behind their table a crack in the wall, the entrance to the Last Crevasse bar. Wait staff bustled through the narrow rift, taking orders and delivering drinks. The hum of conversation washed against the stone and rippled back again, white noise fraying the edges of Holst's attention. The oxygen scrubbers moaned as they struggled to process the gathering carbon dioxide, but no-one else seemed bothered by the low-grade headache from too little O2 in the air, or the sour bludgeon of body odor.

Holst didn't let on that she'd noticed either. "I should buy you a drink," Breech said.

He wiped his face with a kerchief, blotted his sweat-slicked neck. He'd been thinner when they first met, but the years had made him older, heavier, and florid.

Holst studied the landscape outside. "It's kinda pretty," she said.

If Breech noticed, he pretended otherwise. "The beer's good," he said. "Not great, but drinkable. You want?"

"Vodka," Holst said.

"They make it out of soy, this part of the 'Verse."

"Vodka," Holst repeated.

Breech signaled a waitress. The Last Crevasse served drink in stainless-steel canisters, accompanied by two steel cups. Condensation gathered like sweat against the sides.

Breech poured while Holst focused the broken ridges in the distance. They looked like crude, serrated blades hewing their way through the crust of the planet. "What's the survival time on the surface?" she asked.

Breech nudged a glass her way. "Short, I'm guessing."

Holst downed the vodka in a single hit, welcomed the burn in her stomach. Said nothing.

Breech wasn't built for silence. "My brother," he said, then hesitated. Like he'd started the thought and didn't want to finish it, giving himself away for the sake of filling the emptiness. Holst tilted her head back, watched him, waiting. Breech fidgeted, took a deep breath.

"My brother used to have nightmares about that sort of thing," he said. "Getting sucked through an airlock accidentally, or getting dumped out on the surface of a planet hostile to life. Used to say it wasn't dying that bothered him, it was that time you knew what was coming and couldn't do a damn thing to stop it. All those empty seconds when you absolutely know you're fucked."

"Huh."

Breech blotted his face again. He signaled for the waitress and ordered a water. "Rest of the vodka's yours," he said.

Holst nodded. Drank.

"It tastes wrong." Breech shook his head. "Fucking soy beans."

The waitress brought out another steel canister, distinguished from the vodka by a thick blue band. Breech unscrewed the top and drained it in a single pull. Holst poured another drink. She didn't taste anything but the familiar, antiseptic burn.

The oxygen scrubbers moaned overhead. A trio of miners emerged from the Last Crevasse, the meaty stench of their sweat trailing along behind them.

"I hate it here," Breech said.

"I know."

"No. I really hate it here." Breech slid a finger along the condensate on his water, rubbed it against his temple in a futile attempt to get cool. "And this job is real simple, E. Nothing rough. Not really. Just go in, loom a little. Put the fear of god into a bunch of colony yokels."

Holst looked at the rough walls of the complex. She studied the landscape outside. Breech wasn't talking about a gig Tolland approved of.

"Easy money," he said. "Enough for both of us to buy out our contracts. Two hours' work, max, even if the caca hits the fan. Catch the first flight into orbit, make a jump to somewhere civilized, easy as fucking anything."

"You ever have anyone tell you that and actually have it be true?" Holst said.

"Sure." Breech spread his hands, smiling. "All the fucking time, yeah? Things go right a whole lot more than they go wrong, E. It's just we're built to remember the fuck-ups."

"Huh."

"All the fucking time," Breech insisted. "Only reason we live out here, in the middle of all this, is 'cause shit goes right, every day, without us even noticing."

Holst drank.

"And people get paid for easy shit," Breech said. "Same as they get paid for the shit that goes wrong."

Holst looked at the canisters, one half-full of soy-bean vodka and the other left with nothing but a small dribble of water. She ran her finger along the rim of her cup, picked it up and tested its weight.

"Median survival time on the surface is about sixty seconds," Holst said. "There's all sorts of shit that will kill you on the wrong side of an airlock. Lack of pressure means your bodily fluids aren't going to stay liquid like they should. All your tissue is going to expand to levels that aren't compatible with ongoing life. Temperature extremes will flay you alive. It's a bad way to go."

Breech glanced out the bubble port, kerchief against his neck. "Minutes a long time," he said. "My brother's right to worry, yeah?"

"No." Holst adjusted her grip on the cup, fingers curving around the steel. "Thing is, you're only conscious for ten, fifteen seconds of it thanks to the oxygen deprivation. Your thinking will get all kinds of foggy before you hit that point. The window you've got to process what's happening is shorter than you'd think. After that's gone, you're hoping there's someone else to save you, 'cause you're not doing shit to stop the inevitable."

She focused her attention on Breech. "Basically, you don't

get more than a handful of seconds to process how fucked you are," she said. "Your brother's worried about the wrong thing."

Breech met her stare. He was a big man, but Holst was bigger in every way that counted. Taller, heavier, muscle and scar tissue.

"Shit," Breech said.

"Yeah."

"What did I—"

"Your last gig," Holst said.

"You're kidding."

She shrugged. "It wasn't clean and easy. Neither were the two before that."

Breech closed his eyes and processed. "It was the fucking bottom level of this shit," he said. "Unregistered nobodies. It's not a big deal."

"You went freelance," Holst said. "You left bodies behind."

"They weren't nobody," Breech said. "No way they get linked to me."

"I figured it out," Holst said. "You're ambitious and you're sloppy, and that's a bad combination. Tolland wants you off his crew."

"Tolland shipped me here to do what I've been doing."

"No," Holst said. "He brought you here to do a job. You signed a contract, and you broke it."

Breech rose slowly, seat scrapping the stone floor. Holst stood with him. The wind pushed dust across the landscape outside, small clouds scudding hard and fast.

"Sit down," Holst said.

"You could let me go," Breech said.

Holst nodded. "I could," she said.

"You could get me to a shuttle, let me off planet and no-one will be the wiser."

Holst shifted her weight and said nothing.

"It's a big galaxy," Breech said. "Man could find all sorts of ways to get lost where he won't be found again. No-one needs to know at all. No-one needs to know a damn thing. Tolland isn't going to want a report, right? He's just going to take your nod and no-one will speak of shit again?"

"Yes," Holst said.

"Put me in a suit and let me walk," Breech said. "Let me—"

He watched her face, trying to read it. She gave him nothing.

"I've got money," he said. "A little stashed away. Enough to make it worth your while."

Holst sat down again. She nodded at Breech's chair. "You'll want to pull that close," she said.

He moved cautiously. Twitchy. Not sure that he'd really convinced her of anything. That was okay. Holst wanted him fretting.

"Do you know how you screwed up?"

Breech shook his head, mutely.

"Details," Holst said. "Attention to details. You get ninety percent of everything down, then forget about the important stuff."

Breech made a small noise in the back of his throat and looked at the wait staff heading in and out of the Last Crevasse. Searching for an opening that would let him run. Holst let him look. He wasn't going anywhere.

"You can't do me here," Breech said. "Too many witnesses."

"Okay," she said. "Let's assume that's true."

Breech slouched back in his chair, dropped one hand below the tabletop. "You're not going to do me with witnesses. You already thinking of letting me walk?"

"Not how this works," Holst said.

"It could be."

No. Breech didn't get it. Holst poured two fingers of vodka into her cup, feigned ignorance of the hand Breech inched towards his blade. Stupid. Breech eyed the steel vodka bottle. Did the math. Could she do enough damage with it to stop him? Should he risk the knife now, or wait for an opening.

Their waitress collected the empty water canister. "Is everything okay?" she said.

"Sure," Holst said. "We're great."

The waitress nodded at the vodka. "You done with that?"

"No," Holst said.

Breech didn't miss it. He placed his left hand on the tabletop, ready to push himself out of the chair.

"What about you?" the waitress asked. Easy, pleasant, just doing her job. Breech blinked, switching gears.

"Yeah, I'm done," he said, uncertainly. He looked up, smiling, confident. Picking his moment.

Holst stood as he turned back. Took a step left, cutting off his way out. People sifted through the closely packed tables, drunking to erase their cares.

Even with the knife Breech knew he was done. Holst could see it in his face.

He said, "you know, I really hate it here."

"It's an easy place to hate."

"You ain't made to be out here, E. No more than I am," Breech said.

Holst smiled. They'd all discovered life on the colony less fun than they'd been advised, the stakes in Tolland's business too little to pay off in a meaningful way. It changed nothing. Business was still business, orders were still orders.

"Put the knife away," she said.

He didn't. Breech lunged. Four seconds from the thought to the moment it sank in that his blade wasn't going to make contact with flesh.

Holst dodged right, let the cup fall from her fingers. It dropped and bounced off the hard floor, clattering as vodka splattered across their shoes. Breech's attention followed the it down, giving into instinct.

It gave her three seconds before he corrected, re-adjusted his balance and got the knife between them. The first second had the vodka flask in hand, two-thirds drunk and pleasingly heavy at the base. The next two seconds added centrifugal force to her swing. She connected, hard and sharp, with the soft part of Breech's temple.

Skin split open. Blood splattered the table and stone floor. Breech dropped to one knee, half-blind and hurting. Snarled as he rose and came at her again.

Instinct and training took over after that. Hers were better than his.

WARM MILK & WHISKEY

Baby Lulu was all kinds of funny-looking, with the too big head and the too smart eyes, gadding about in the cybernetic crèche with a frame like one of burnt-out wrestlers who turned mook for the Cabots. He'd stare at you sometimes, the way infants do, part of his brain still figuring out the world and trying to pull two-and-two together. Still young and chubby, legs plump as sausages in the fluid of the crèche. It was criminal the way his old man hyper-evolved the kid, let alone found him a spot in the goddamned police force.

They stuck Lulu with me because the chief was still ten kinds of pissed about the incident at the Christmas party. And we closed cases together, me and Baby Lulu. Whatever genius drove the kid's old man to be part of the mad science brigade, cloning dinosaurs and building rockets strong enough to fly to Venus, he got things right sometimes. Baby Lulu showed the same knack for brilliance when it came to solving murders.

Too bad that made the wrong kind of people angry. Too bad they were the kind of folks who kept half the force in their pocket.

"McGinty tried to write Gracie Steppard's death off as suicide," Baby Lulu said as the bartender warmed his milk. "The woman has seven stab wounds in her back." The crèche threw up its cybernetic arms to emphasis the point.

"McGinty knows where his bread is buttered," I said, nursing my whisky. "Steppard was mixed up with Jamie Cabot."

"You're saying McGinty is on the take?"

"Or he's trying to avoid seven stab wounds in his own back," I said. "Cabot isn't a man known for his rational response to being provoked."

"It's bullshit, is what it is," Lulu said, and accepted his milk from the barman. The kid sucked on the nipple, contemplating the case. He liked to drink and think.

Me, I was content to drink and try to forget my troubles. Smart as he was, working the job, there were still days when Baby Lulu reminded you he was so damn young. Eighteen months old and figuring out the world, his lack of experience mitigated by the AI in his crèche. They said it was his developing brain, guiding the AI, that allowed for the intuitive leap. Maybe that was bullshit, and it was just the AI that did all the thinking while the kid was along for the ride.

I don't know. Mad science isn't my beat, but there was genius in there somewhere. And Baby LuLu's old man was an optimist. That tended to filter into the kid's world-view. It never occurred to him criminals like Cabot were anything other than black hats, and therefore destined to lose in any clash with the police.

I pushed my half-drunk glass away, done with it. What I'd already drunk roiled in my gut, sour and heavy with dark promises.

"I don't get it," Baby Lulu said. "What makes a cop like McGinty fall in with a man like Cabot?"

He turned his innocent baby blues on me. Sucked on his milk and waited.

"People turn for stupid reasons, really." I scrubbed my wrist against my neck. "It's all just leverage and base instincts."

"How so?"

I couldn't meet his eyes anymore. "People have secrets they want to keep hidden. Or Cabot threatened his family. Maybe it's just medical bills, and insurance doesn't cover shit."

The stupid, fat cheeks went taut. "Maybe McGinty wanted the money."

"Maybe," I said. "It happens."

"What about you?" Baby Lulu said. "What would it take for Cabot to lure a cop like you to the dark side, Palmer?"

My hackles rose at the question, wondering how the Kid had figured things out. I thought I'd played things so careful, but when they partner you with an infant genius…

I decided to play it cool. "Money wouldn't do it."

"But something could, if a man like Cabot was determined."

"A man like Cabot can do most things, if he sets his mind to it," I said. "Finish your drink. Maude's expecting me home, and I want to see the girls before they got to bed."

We left the bar together, and at first I thought the kid had my whole plan figured out. He nudged me away from the alley out back, where I might have put a bullet in him and dumped the body near the trash from the Seven Dragon's restaurant. Avoided a short-cut through the park, where I might have found a quiet spot with plenty of ways to get clear after the pistol shot rang out.

Games within games, you know what I'm saying? I figured the kid knew and planned to get me before I could get in. Thinking about it made my nerves all fluttery, and I wondered if I could talk myself out of what had to be done.

I didn't. Cabot had made the price clear, and Maude's life was worth more to me than some billionaire scientists freak show offspring.

Still, weird as he was, Baby Lulu was still a kid. Smarter and stronger than any toddler, in his thrice-damned crèche, but he only knew a little bit about the world that he hadn't learned from books.

And that included that sixth sense that tells you when to trust someone, and when to read the room and realize something's up. We ended up walking along the path by the river, heading up to the station. The one that went down and under Lumen's Bridge, where it's dark and the steep embankment would disguise exactly where a gun had been fired in the shadows.

It should have been so easy. Pull the Smith and Wesson and put a bullet in that big, gawky, over-sized, awkward head.

But Baby Lulu turned to me, fixed me with those big blue eyes. He said, "I don't think you're right, Palmer. I don't think Cabot could get to you."

"Yeah? Why's that?"

"You're a good man," Baby Lulu said. "And a damned good cop. I look forward to learning from you, over the next few years."

Hell of a thing to say, right before what needed to happen. But I thought about the letter in my mailbox, the few locks of Maude's hair that accompanied the instructions and the warnings about what they'd send next if Baby Lulu wasn't eliminated.

"A man like you finds a way," Baby Lulu said. "He doesn't let scum like Cabot paint him into a corner, I don't think."

I'll never know if he said it innocently, or because he'd twigged that I would falter. But I know the resolve went out of me, and my gun stayed in its holster. All I could do was pray it was the right choice, and Baby Lulu really was as good at the job as I hoped.

"Kid, I got to tell you about this letter," I said. "And I'm going to need your help taking care of a little problem."

THE FUCKING-SHITFULL-GODDAMNED-ASSHOLE-NOODLECOCKED-MOTHERFUCKER HAS TO DIE

Gail double-checked the twelve-gauge and slid it back into the shoulder holster, then put hands to wheels and rolled her way across the Waycross Road. For week's she'd been listening to the sorcerers bang upon about the great enemy, an ancient evil they refused to name for fear it would track them down. Gail and the other servants had never quite jibed with the portentous replacement titles, and referred to him by artful arrangements of profanity instead. Lise was always the best at it—the mouth on that woman could curdle milk with blistering bursts of foul language—and when they were in private, Lise delighted in finding profane combinations that would double Gail over with laughter.

The Seven Sorcerers were dead now, as were Lise and all the others. Someone had said the name out loud, and that Fucking-Shitfull-Goddamned-Asshole-Noodlecocked-Motherfucker had breached their defenses and unleashed hell when everybody had their guard down. Gail was one of the few survivors, and she would not take that lying down.

Lise deserved better, even if all the Seven Sorcerers were shitty fuckers only marginally better than their ancient foe. And it wasn't like the Motherfucker was hard to find if you were looking. Just follow the trail of bats and rats and bad feelings through the city, and you'd eventually stumble across one of those brownstones that was so shielded with wards and glamours it triggered a headache if you crossed the street out front.

A few pedestrians flashed Gail a wary look as she rolled her chair across the street, but nobody said boo about the weapon. She figured they either failed to see it, too focused on the chair, or the brownstone's defenses were already working upon her, reaching out to discourage interest in the woman making a beeline for the front door.

Magic cut both ways sometimes, even if it took an iron will and a handful of aspirin to ward off the headache that came with pushing back and rolling to the stairs.

There were eleven steps between the street and the brownstone's front door. Hard to climb when rolling solo, but nothing insurmountable. Gail backed her wheels up and reached up the rail to give herself leverage, tipped back to find her leverage and worked her way up, step-by-step. The front door was locked and dead-bolted, but the motherfucker hadn't bothered with additional wards, so it took her less than a minute to pick them both and roll on inside.

She drew the twelve-gauge and held it across her lap, running a hand against the stock. The gun had belonged to Edmund Nicodemus, the member of the seven they called the Gun Mage. A shitty sorcerer, but he knew his firearms. There were runes etched down the barrel, and they glowed softly in the dim light. The Motherfucker's wards probably picked up the gun as a bigger threat than Gail, even if the damn thing was harmless without someone to pull the trigger. Mages were just like every other motherfucker, pig-ignorant and verging on stupid when estimating what could be done from a chair.

Gail tried to call out, but on her first attempt, her voice came out in a squeak thanks to the nerves clawing at her throat. She coughed and drew a deep breath, forced herself to calm. Dropped her voice down an octave for the second attempt, and bellowed from deep in her gut.

"Hey, asshole, you killed a friend of mine. Get your goddamned-bitch-ass-behind down here and—"

The Motherfucker appeared on at the balcony rail on the second floor, stepping out of the shadows to make an entrance like some B-Movie vampire portrayed by Bela Lugosi. Gail craned her neck back and pointed. "Yeah, you, motherfucker. Get your fucking ass down here so I can fuck you up."

It sounded hollow to her ears, more bravado than bravery, but all Gail's fear evaporated the moment the Motherfucker grinned that overconfident, condescending, grin and flowed down the stairs like a cloud of fast-moving darkness gathered around a pale, cruel, balding head and two hands with long, bronze-clawed fingers.

"You!" The Motherfucker crowed. "What would one such as I have to fear from a weak, insignificant worm like you, girl? I am the great best of the dark, the conquering worm that will lay waste to the world. I am—"

He liked to monologue, which wasn't a surprise. All the Seven Sorcerers could bang on for hours about their greatness. Difference was, they paid Gail and the rest damn well to put up with the monologuing. They paid otherwise logical people to endure their rules and bullshit instead of doing what made sense. She didn't owe the Motherfucker any kind of audience, so she raised the twelve gauge and pulled the trigger as he hit the bottom of the stairs.

Gold-flecked shot spat out the barrel and winged him as the Motherfucker tried to spin away. The impact kicked him back —Nicodemus messed with the laws of physics around the gun after watching too many action movies—but it didn't put the Motherfucker down. He surged towards her, lunging for the weapon, and tried to reef it out of her hands.

No dice there. One thing you could say about the chair — you built up hella arm muscles and off-the-chart grip strength. Sorcery did the opposite—not one of the Seven was worth a damn in a hand-to-hand fight. Gail wrestled for control, the chair jerking up on one wheel as the Motherfucker tried to leverage the gun and topple her over.

She focused on getting the gun twisted, pointed up and at the Motherfucker's face.

"This is for Lise," she said.

At close range, the gold-flecked shot and magically enhanced kick of its impact made one hell of a mess of the Motherfucker's head. His corpse flew across the room, shadows dissipating as he crunched against a wood-paneled wall.

Gail rolled over and spat on the headless corpse. The lingering headache from the house's wards dissipated as the Motherfucker's blood stained the floorboards black.

Should have done that fucking weeks ago, but no, the Seven weren't up for that. Always sure they knew what was best, never willing to listen to an alternate point of view or perspective on life.

Gail waited there for an hour, gun at the ready, in case he respawned. Unlike the Seven, she'd seen a movie or two instead of living nose-deep in arcane tomes and mouldering books of forgotten law. She knew how this shit worked, and she wanted to be sure it was done.

Somewhere, on the other side, she hoped it brought Lise's soul a little peace.

THIS IS HOW YOU STEP UP

Brad drove rally cars before the Mist, circling dirt tracks at high speed in a lime green V8 Holden. My high speed driving experience consisted of too much *Grand Theft Auto,* so the division of labor worked out easy. Brad sat behind the wheel, foot jammed against the accelerator, and I spend every delivery in our makeshift tail gunner's perch. Brad always claims gunner's a better job—no responsibility, all the firepower—but Brad's not the one strapped into a seat watching the landscape roll past the back of his skull. Driver has all the control in a dust runner crew, and the gunner plays second fiddle.

Brad's humility plays well with the ladies, though. He ain't shy about exploiting that.

His latest squeeze, a babe name Laura, hooked us up with Old Man Ekmo. Escorted us into Ekmo's lair, an old pool hall on Boundary Road, and hyped us for a last-minute gig.

Ekmo Nunes laid out the job. "I need a crew for a Warwick run," he rasped. "Get it done in three hours, and I'll pay extra."

Brad preened, eager for the cred that came with pulling this off.

That meant I had to be the smart one. "When do we leave?" I said.

"ASAP."

"What's the cargo?"

"Not your concern."

Shady, yes, but that's the business, and dust runners survive on their rep.

Brad flashed a thumbs up. "Fuck man, this sounds like fun."

Laura leant through the driver's side window to deliver one last kiss for luck. "Be fast," she said. "Be safe."

"Darlin, you don't gotta worry," Brad said. "This is what we do."

I clipped myself into the tail gunners perch, wishing I could slap him. We'd caught this run in the last days of summer, when the sun dragged a slow, savage arc across the sky. My ass melted against the vinyl seat we'd welded to the tray of our ute. The big .50 caliber M2 was already warm to touch, twin belts of ammo hooked in place. Survey said I'd sweat my balls off, even if nothing else took us out.

I dropped my goggles in place and hooked a bandanna over my mouth. Thumped one hand against the hot steel. "We're on the clock," I shouted, and Brad came up for air.

"You'll have to excuse us, Darlin'," he said. "Time to make some dosh."

Three ways a BrisVegas-to-Warwick run goes sideways— dinos, raiders, and Mist. You outrun the dinos, outgun the raiders, and accept your fate if the Mist envelopes you. Every dust runner knows the odds, and we still roll the dice.

We picked up the Hell Riders just outside of Ipswich, thirty minutes into the run. One minute we're the only thing on the road, doing ninety down the dust-choked highway. The next, we had company—two dozen armed fuckers on dirt bikes hooting and hollering threats as they roared down the highway.

Stories pegged the Hell Riders as cannibals, eager to chow down on a leg *and* make off with your cargo. Can't swear that's true, but I'd buy it. No other reason to chase a runner crew at the start of their goddamned job, and we were booking fast enough to suspect the ute was running light.

I signaled Brad, and he floored it, left half the Riders eating our dust. The other half kept coming, closing the distance. Guns out, firing wild, howling threats I couldn't make out over the whistling wind. Persistent fuckers with something to prove, or a hunger to be satiated.

I put my hands on the big .50 cal and grinned. Time to earn my cut.

Dust-running 101: don't shoot to kill if you don't need to. Rookie gunners freak at the first sign of pursuit, hold down the trigger until the belts run dry and the barrel overheats. They're focused on eliminating pursuers, and figure more bullets means more bodies. Rookie gunners are idiots; they blow three hundred rounds with fuck all gain. It's hard enough to spray-and-pray when the machine gun's not in motion. Shit's ten times harder when you're bouncing down the highway, your driver weaving to avoid return fire. A smart gunner focuses on deterrence, doing just enough to coax their pursuers into fighting another day. Smart gunners pick their spots, then unleash short bursts of hell. Maximum impact, minimal ammo wasted.

My first burst hit the Hell Riders while they clumped together, bullets chewing through bikes and flesh alike. Three fell, and the rest split in half, coming at us on either flank. Smart play, making themselves smaller targets, and some gunners might get rattled. Not me—I'd dealt with smarter raiding parties, and my next burst chewed through the front tire of the Hell Rider coming up on the right. He wobbled, then spun out of control. Avoiding the carnage sent the rider behind him careening off the highway.

The staccato pop handguns fired over handlebars answered my burst. Less accurate than my .50 cal, but I had a dozen targets and they had one. A bullet ripped a hole in the aluminium tray six inches from my foot. Another ricocheted off the roll bars we'd built around my perch. Both sent a chill deep into my guts, but plenty of folks shoot at me these days. I can persevere.

A Hell Rider with a flame-red Mohawk crept up on the left. I swung the .50 cal in his direction and cut him in two with a close-range burst, transformed the rider into a cloud of mist left behind by a riderless Kawasaki. Brad leaned on the accelerator, gained another hundred meters. Then another hundred more.

The surviving Hell Riders hit their limit, unable or unwilling to keep up the chase.

Biggest known threat on the Warwick run is the Megalosaurus camped outside Kalbar, an evil fucker the locals dubbed Big Red on account of his blood-streaked hide. Big Red emerged from the Mist a decade back, borged up with cybernetic legs and a thermos-reactor for a heart. Three inches of steel plating covered his vital organs, and his teeth were titanium teeth sharp. No-one's figured out why these bastards emerge transformed into war machines, but we thank our lucky stars nobody bothered to arm the dinos for a long-range fight. Big Red could hit speeds of a hundred and twenty clicks an hour, but you won't get lasered to a crisp or blown off the road with a heat-seeker, just chewed up and spat out.

He caught wind of our engine and gave chase as we tore down Highway 15, and my gun done fuck all to deter him. Hot shell casing fell like savage rain, left burn marks on my legs, and I grit my teeth and kept on firing, 'cause what else did I have? Brad put pedal to metal, barely in control of the ute. We slid and swerved in the dust, and I thought we might roll a few times. My balls crawled up inside my body and my mouth got pasty with fear, but I peppered Red with short, futile bursts. If he blinked, it'd buy us a few extra meters, and every gain counted against a dino.

On a straight line, we were toast, but an armored dinosaur Big Red's size and weight can't take tight turns for shit, and Brad wasn't afraid to roll off-track and use a few sliding turns to shake the big dino loose. We'd pulled that trick a few times, making the run in the past.

No dice this time round. Big Red tumbled our strategy and changed his game plan on the fly. A big leg punting an abandoned Ford pickup, launching the rust-streaked wreck like a missile. It sailed up and over, whistling as it fell to earth, and Brad swerved hard to avoid the target zone. Big Red unleashed a roar of triumph and booted a second car, and I fired up the .50 Cal again, hoping to throw off his aim.

Evasive maneuvers took a toll, and Big Red closed our lead. Got so close every roar washed fetid breath over my tail-gunner's perch, and his teeth weren't six meters from my feet.

Good news for us: Big Red's teeth were steel, but his gums were flesh. I sprayed bullets the moment he gave me a soft target. Fifty caliber rounds gashed bloody wounds in Big Red's soft palate, and the big guy crashed hard, sparks flying as his amour scraped against the road.

We hadn't killed him—Big Red staggered upright as Brad tore off—but he wasn't catching up.

I'd burned through our ammo in the attempt to hold Big Red at bay, damn near melting the gun to slag chewing through so many bullets. Our back-up plan was a 12 gauge and the Beretta at my hip, neither of which were great options.

Fuck it. I crawled of the harness and scrambled for the cab. Brad caught my approach in the rearview, and I signaled my plan to enter. It ain't easy clambering through the passenger side window when you're doing ninety-five on the straight, but it wasn't my first attempt. Practice dulled the sheer, bloody minded panic.

Nothing beats sitting passenger side on a run. The tail-gunner's perch is all wind and dust and discomfort, unable to picture what's ahead. Passengers just deal with the engine's grumble and the soft lull of Brad's favorite cassettes, Elvis Presley crooning songs about Vegas and girls and true love.

"How we doing for time?" I said.

"Big Red cost us a few minutes, but we're on track to earn our bonus."

"Even if we gotta re-arm at Warwick?"

"Even then," Brad said.

We bumped fists. "Twenty minutes to Warwick." Brad grinned over the steering wheel. "Fifteen if we book it."

We laughed it up, cracking jokes, already spending our bonus money.

Then the fucking Mist settled around us, because god lives to punish hubris.

Some people disappear into the mist, replaced by dinos like Big Red. Some people emerged unscathed, except for a little confusion about how long they were trapped inside. Near as we know, there's no way to tip the balance. All you can do is pray and keep moving, trying to find a way out. Brad had the wheel, so I got prayer.Given the choice, I would have gone back to firing fifty-cal rounds at Big Red's armor in a goddamned heartbeat—it felt a lot less futile.

Brad flicked on the high beams, hunching forward to keep eyes on the road. Elvis asked for a love both tender and true, but his crooned request felt like sacrilege. Asking for anything but deliverance tempted fate, so I killed the stereo and kept my mouth shut. For the next half-hour we rolled on, breath caught in our throats, nothing to do but watch the strange lights flash and chaotic eddies in the Mist.

"This shit goes on forever," Brad said.

"Just keep driving. We'll make it clear."

"Ya think"

I didn't.

"Sure," I said. Hope's not the greatest tactic, but what else did we have?

Two hours later, the Mist thinned and our visibility improved. Brad pushed on, accelerating into the bright summer afternoon, shooting out of the clinging Mist like a cork pushed from a bottle. We skidded to a halt, and in the rearview, the Mist evaporated. The road behind us looked familiar, edged by gum trees, prickly pear, and overgrown farmland long abandoned.

Brad let out a holler of victory, punching the steering wheel with the sheer joy of it. I exhaled a long breath and nodded. It seemed we'd come through unscathed.

Brad kept an old compass in the glove box, alongside some paper maps. Best he figured, we'd overshot Warwick by fifty klicks, but it weren't no thing to loop back. Twenty minutes on the road, he said. Piece of fucking piss.

We took off, giddy as heck: We'd survived the fucking Mist!

Our relief lasted until we rolled into town and realized Warwick hadn't shared our fate.

The pickup was on Dragon Street, just around the corner from the refugee camp set up when raiders and dinos hit the smaller towns out west. The address was an old Queenslander huddled against a corner block, the overgrown backyard dotted with massive sheds held shut with rusting padlocks. Brad and I collected handguns, just in case.

We shouldn't have bothered.

Half-drunk cups of tea dotted the living room, lukewarm. Dog food covered the kitchen floor, alongside a shattered plate. Empty outfits everywhere, ragged shirts and stained jeans, Blundstone boots with socks inside 'em. No insects or bird calls, no ambient signs of life. The Mist had scoured Warwick bare.

"Man," I said. "Ekmo's going to be pissed."

Brad eased into the master bedroom, gun held at the ready. "Come on. He can't blame us for this, can he?"

"I think the fact he's Ekmo Nunes means he can blame us for whatever the fuck he wants."

Brad slowed to a stop. That train of thought had led him to some nasty, inevitable stations, and he didn't enjoy the possible stops further down the line.

"We could bail," he said. "Fuck off south, head down Sydney way for a stretch. I hear they always need good courier teams."

"We got the gas to make it past Byron?"

"Nah."

"Not the best plan, then."

"Nah, guess not."

Our second sweep of the house focused on contraband and concealed stashes of ammo and supplies. Good salvage can redeem a fucked up run and part of me hoped we'd stumble over the hidden cargo Ekmo Nunes wanted. Secrecy worked against him, and sixty minutes turned up bupkis. Whatever contraband Ekmo bought, the suppliers took their secrets into the mist and left us empty-handed.

Brad threw a right at the nearest wall. Back home, it would have been cheap plaster, easy enough to put your fist through. Out Warwick way, in an old Queenslander, he hit the painted hardwood wall with all his weight behind it. Broke three fingers and his wrist.

Brad howled. Idiot. I dredged up my 5th grad first-aid training and splinted Brad's hand. Ignored the deranged internal rant laying out all the ways he'd screwed us. No percentage in saying this shit out loud. Brad—like all great drivers—is bravado packed around a porcelain-fragile ego. Great when they can get up and go, useless once they're hedged in.

Brad bitched about his fucked-up hand, then waxed lyrical about Laura's ass as a prelude to bemoaning he'd never see her again. He moved on to the tragedy of being stuck, how we'd never get to boast about this run and pick up work off the rep. "We survived the fucking Mist," he said. "We could write our own damn ticket."

I pumped Brad full of painkillers, quietly pondering the actual problems: getting home without a driver; talking Ekmo Nunes into forgiving us for showing up empty-handed; avoiding Big Red and the Hell Riders both, without a gunner to discourage 'em.

"We're doomed," Brad said. "I can't drive like this."

"Good thing there's two of us."

"I've seen you drive," Brad said. "We're still fucked."

"Shouldn't have shattered your hand, then."

"Ha," Brad said. The drugs were kicking in, and his head lolled to one side. "Seemed like an idea, yeah?"

Ihoisted him upright, walked the stone fucker back to the ute. Strapped his protesting ass into the passenger seat and rummaged his pocket for the keys.

"Don't," he said, weakly. "Mattie, don't."

Then, rather sensibly, he passed the fuck out.

I climbed behind the wheel and got a feel for the spot. Adjusted the rearview, moved the seat forward. Spared a glance for the dormant .50 Cal bolted to the back . Didn't seem so different to being back there, really. Driver made the choices that got you into trouble; tail gunner did their best to keep the fuckery at bay, buying time to pull off the win.

I caught my face in the rearview, dust-streaked and red around the pale patches where the goggles covered my eyes. Creases around my eyes pulling tight, like I didn't want nobody to see just how scared I was to get driving, or dealing with Ekmo Nunes back home.

Piss on that, though. No reason to stop. One thing the tail gun teaches you: fear doesn't mean you quit trying, otherwise everyone's dead. Brad mumbled something and twisted in the passenger seat, smooshing his cheek against the window.

"You can do this," I said. A little promise to myself. "This is how you step up."

Then I fired up the engine and drove.

THE FIGHTER

Triss hunches over, eyes screwed shut to block out the sodium yellow of the locker room's fluorescents. She's already a mass ofinjuries: stitches above her right eye; ribs battered to a yellow-green consistency; knuckles turned into black, misshapen things from a full tournament of throwing fists against steel. They aren't supposed to let humans fight in these tourneys, but they won't let Triss fight humans anymore.

And she needs it. The adrenaline, the freedom to walk out there and throw down against the best.

Still, every part of her aches now. Triss figures she's broken bones, mushed cartridge, damaged muscle.

And part of her thinks she's done far worse to the parts of her that aren't governed by flesh.

———

P3-83 the Mangler screams across the ring and smashes Triss with a titanium fist. She rolls with it, sweat spraying across the plastic barricade. A soft ooh of anticipation as the crowd registers the impact.

Triss spits blood and brings up her guard. She's scouted the robot. Truss scouts everyone. The organisers think she's a sideshow, a spectacle to beat up in the first round. She knows what they're all thinking now: Poor little cyborg girl with a prosthetic heart and a steel leg, trying to pretend she can hold her own against a robot built for battle.

None of them knew how good Triss was before the accident. They don't know how bad she needs to make this work.

P3-83 circles on spindled legs, eight of them working like a spider. Great for balance and short, sharp movement. Triss wipes her mouth and spits blood, soaks in the bay of the crowd.

She knows the robot's program, has studied the way he drops low and comes in when he sees an opening.

And she knows exactly where to batter the damn thing to ensure the chassis dents and breaks…

———

Triss curls over, fighting the pain. Bodie argues it's time to quit. They're three bouts in, three winner's purses delivered and signed off. No need to destroy herself any further.

"It's not about the money," she tells him.

Bodie shakes his head. "Then what in fuck is it about, kid?"

She squints at him through swollen eyes. Bodie's old now, grey and weathered beneath his worn black cap. Against this from the start, but still willing to train her and be in the corner.

"Just get me up and fighting," she says. "Get me through the last match."

———

CMP-1 started life as an industrial 'bot, hauling supplies on and off freighter ships. A heavyweight beast of a robot, built for power and durability. Triss hammers at the big, heavy torso because CMP-1's last opponent worked it hard. There's dents there, and a small gap where a seam of metal has split and peeled. Her best chance of taking the 'bot down is getting that open, finding access to the delicate circuitry inside, and all she's got to do is stay on her feet and avoid the big, sweeping haymakers that could take her head off with one strike.

It takes longer than she expected for CMP-1 to figure out that Triss is faster and more agile, and he switches from throwing punches to body checking her with the full weight of the big, industrial chassis. The impact sends her sprawling and Triss tastes blood in her mouth, every part of her stunned by the impact and struggling to recover.

Her vision swims, refusing to focus. But the adrenaline kicks in as she makes out the raw bulk of CMP-1 approaching, and knows there's a bit fist swinging down to take Triss out of the fight. She rolls towards the barricade, uses the wall to get back to a vertical base.

CMP-1 comes in, hoping to trap her against the wall, and she weaves left to avoid the first fist, flits right to avoid the second.

She sees her opening and takes it, punches a fist through the seam and crunches it against a mass of wiring.

Triss grabs hold and rips for all she's worth, praying that she's got something vital…

———

"I can shoot your hands full of painkillers," Bodie says. "Splint the bones with steel supports, because they ain't going do shit about that here. It'll slow you down a little, steal some power from your jab. Nothing you can't work around, normally, but theres nothing normal about this. You aren't a robot, Triss. Fatigue's going to get to you the way it won't affect him."

"Do it," Triss says. "Don't worry about meat sack."

"I will fuckin' worry about the meat, love. If I don't, there's a good chance you'll lose more of it after all this."

"As if that's such a bad thing," Triss says.

———

Bertram Razor is just like her, a cyborg, but there's damn little flesh remaining in the big heavyweight's hulking frame. Steel jaw, steel arms, steel leg, armoured chest. Spine rewired with titanium rods to support the extra weight. Tricker than all the others, because there's a human brain driving all that metal.

But that brain was a street brawler, untrained and unproven. Good against the 'bots because it adapted in situations not covered by their programming, but Triss thinks faster and has trained herself to be better, even if she's at least 74% more flesh and still qualifies as human.

She comes at him hard and fast, targets the fleshy leg and the fleshy ears still capable of registering pain. Welters the cyborg with all she's got, and she can see the fear in the too-human eyes above the razor-sharp jawline.

Poor bastard has no chance when she goes in for the kill. Puts him down and mounts him, raining down punches.

"This is what I do," she screams, punctuating each new blow. "THIS IS WHAT I DO."

———

It hurts to stand, despite the drugs, and Triss uses Bodie's shoulder to hold herself steady. One last fight, and she's done with the tournament. One last fight, and she's proved she measures up, better than the best they've programmed and built for the Battle Brawl.

It's small time, a low-level street tourney, but she can build to the bigger things. Replace her aching arms with steel, just like Bertram Razar. Replace her clunky cyborg legs with something less bipedal, more useful for finding position and fighting a stick-and-move battle.

This is all about the learning curve, figuring out what needs to change in order to make it in this new arena. To be the very best, since they won't let her prove it in the old rings with flesh and blood opponents.

All she's got to do is survive and get her hand raised. One last fight, and she can do that.

Bodie loops a white towel over his shoulders and gathers up his kit. "I ain't going to let them kill you, kid. I ain't going to let it go that far."

She reaches for the towel, and fumbles it. Her fingers too numb to really do anything but make a fist and throw leather in the ring.

Bodie collects the towel and twists it in his hands. The fingers are old, so wrinkled and fragile that Triss wonders if they were ever strong. But he doesn't put it around his neck again, just holds onto it like a talisman when they call her, and the low bass of her fight song start to play, he gets her over to the tunnel and ready to walk out.

"Do what you gotta do, kid," he says, and Triss nods like she'll do just that.

One last fight to prove she's got what it takes, and then the hurting will finally stop.

IT'S NOT A JOB

So it's a Thursday and the three of us, me and Wiki and Cady, smoke cigarettes on the roof before cleaning the twenty-third floor. Our manager would ream our asses if she knew, pitch a fit over the maid service stinking like an ashtray, but Cady wanted a smoke and she's got this way about her. She'll get jack of working and declare a smoke break, and somehow we end up on the roof and bum smokes even though Wiki says he's quit. The three of us wasting time in the shadow of the Hotel sign bolted up there. The big one, each letter sixteen feet high and luminous in the dark.

So we're smoking when the storm rolls in, these dark, heavy clouds that boil and curl like ink poured into water. Weather that shifts the mood from "what a nice day" to "dear lord, forgive us our trespasses" in the space of a shared cigarette and the short exposition of Wiki's bullshit theories 'bout how the Raiders will do this season.

Cady eyes the clouds with suspicion. "Where the hell did those came from?"

"Warm, damp air rising fast and releasing latent heat as they condense," Wiki says. "You know, like any other cloud."

"Brain that size, and you still rock the mullet." Cady finishes her cigarette and flicks it into the tin we keep up there to store her butts. "Some days, you worry me, big man."

Me, I'm staring at the clouds while they bicker, trying to scratch the itchy tingle out of my arm and ignore the little voice in the back of my head screaming *yo, yo, yo, man, there's something hella wrong here.* Trying to convince myself that sometimes a cloud is just a cloud, and the biggest risk the storm represents is the possibility of being soaked.

Cady is still giving Wiki grief when I finally give in and say, "Guys? Hey guys, yo. I don't think this is just weather, you know?"

The first drop of blood rain falls and splotches against Wiki's cheek. He puts his thick fingers to it and rolls his eyes when they're smeared with crimson.

"This is your fault," he tells me, hauling his big ass off the crate he's been using as a seat.

Cady just gives me this look, like everything would have been fine if I'd just pretended there weren't nothing wrong. Like maybe someone would else would handle things if we took the day off.

We go down to the basement and let Wiki do his thing: chalk circle, candles, long chants in ancient Mesopotamian the rest of us can't even read. His eyes rolled back into his skull as he recites clues in this voice that's not really his. It's all "find the two-headed cockerel in the dark of the fifteenth scorpion moon," same as it ever was, but we've been doing this long enough that it's barely a challenge. Wiki comes out of his trance and puts it all together, figures there's something going down in this warehouse down by the milk factory. Some American ex-pat a-hole who wound up in the south of Mexico trying to introduce Chupacabra to the local ecosystem. The only surprise is the Chupacabra itself, which is bigger than any of us were led to believe. Damn thing has two inches on Wiki when it breaks free of its crate, and it takes all the tranq darts the three of us are carrying to put the damn thing down.

We're all pretty beat-up by the time we make it back. Wiki's got dry blood in his mullet. Cady's a walking bruise and I've got stitches along my gut, where the Chupacabra sliced me open. Our manager gives us holy hell for the twenty-third floor getting done so late and I'm in enough pain that Wiki has to calm me down, keep me from quitting on the spot.

"We got a destiny," he says, "but we still gotta pay rent, dog."

The clouds are still there when we finish up our shift. Me and Wiki study them, but Cady just pulls her jacket tight against the cool wind and says, "don't know about you boys, but I could use a drink."

"I'm in," has left my mouth before I'm really aware of saying it. Wiki gives me a sour look , but fuck it, I've had stitches before. It ain't like getting torn up is a new thing, is it?

We're six vodka tonics in and Cady's eyes are glassy. "This job," she says, nodding slowly. "This job is such a shitty gig."

"You're preaching to the converted here."

"No," she says. "You don't understand. This job is a *really* shitty gig."

"It's not a job, it's a calling."

She lowers her head. Glares at me. We're in this bar down the road from work, this tiny joint with low light and a replica of the Maltese Falcon sitting beside the top-shelf booze. "Don't give me that calling shit," Cady says. "You've got sixteen stitches keeping your damn spleen inside your body."

I flag down a bartender. Order our seventh drink. We're all kinds of flossy by the time they kick us out, and I pull my damn stitches trying to get Cady upstairs and into her own damn bed. We make so much noise that Wiki appears, emerging from his bedroom in boxer shorts, a war-axe in his fist.

"You're bleeding," he says.

"I'm aware."

"You're drunk."

"Aware of that, too." I dump Cady into her unmade bed, pick my way through the piles of dirty laundry until I'm back in the hall with Wiki and the big-ass axe he's toting. "It's getting to her," I tell him. "The job is wearing her down."

"It's not a job," Wiki says. "What we do is a calling."

He says it with a straight face too, like it's something he really believes in.

"Just 'cause something calls you," I say, "it doesn't mean you have to answer."

Cady quits her gig at the hotel the following afternoon. We walk in and the manager gives us grief, re-running the shit-storm she rained down on us pretty much word for word. My stitches hurt and I'm feeling seedy, but I've got the sense to take it. Cady just listens for a few minutes, says she's done with this shit, then walks out on the shift.

It's the first time in over a year we don't end up on the roof. It's the first time in even longer that we can't find her when Wiki receives a vision. We're halfway through cleaning the twenty-first floor when he goes stiff as a board, rattling off warnings in a language I don't speak. Cady's phone rings out. She isn't home when we check there, and she isn't drinking in the usual haunts.

Wiki gets this worried look, like he isn't entirely sure we can do what's needed as a duo. "She was only quitting the hotel, right? She wasn't quitting everything, was she?"

"She can't," I tell him. "We've got a calling. A destiny."

Wiki isn't convinced.

Turns out the the blood rain's the work of this bloke in the sewers, a venerable necromancer-type who started out raising the corpse of his wife for love, then got caught up in the thrill of magic.

I've seen the progression a time or two. One day, you're doing the impossible. Next thing you know, you're raising an army of shambling corpses and trying to appease some elder god, following some prophecy.

Me and Wiki go to work, carving our way through zombies. It's not like it's hard—the undead are pretty fragile, unless you bind the corpse with a demon—but the numbers make it tricky.

One zombie isn't a threat to us, but thirty will get the job done if we lose focus and slip up. Wiki lets himself get bit and spends the rest of the night bitching about needing to stop the infection.

"This never would have happened if Cady hadn't left us," he says. "We shouldn't have let her walk away."

I patch up the bite mark and get him a beer. "Not sure we had a choice in that, mate."

We got up to the roof and study the clear sky, but we find it weird being up there, just the two of us, no cigarettes. Wiki keeps putting his hands in his pockets, then taking them out again. I just sit by the door, kicking my toe against the half-full tin containing our cigarette butts. It occurs to me I'd really, really like something to hit, but my guts are still held together with stitches and there's never something going bump in the night when it's actually useful.

It's four years before I see Cady again. Four years and too many goddamn monsters, not to mention three potential apocalypses and one invasion from a dimension where nightmares are given flesh. When I see her, she's working in a cafe, wearing a crisp black shirt and making espresso in this hippie cafe where male clientele sport lumberjack beards and everyone smells of patchouli oil.

I'm out there staking out this student from the local university that's been calling up Elohim and using them as his own personal agents of vengeance. Wiki has the dormitory covered, going undercover as part of the maintenance crew. I'm on the kid's tail, hoping to find his sanctum, maybe figure out how he's wrangling angels to do his bidding. He goes into this café and orders a latte, and when I see Cady behind the machine, I stop thinking about the job.

Instead, I join the queue. Who gives a crap if this kid is going to see me? I order a long black, and Cady hears my voice. She looks up and smiles and makes my drink. Tells the others behind the counter she's going on break, then escorts me out where she can smoke and pitch butts into a dented tin.

"Damn, kid," she says, "it's good to see you."

"You too," I tell her. "You too."

She smiles and lights up, offers me the pack. I wave it off. "Gave up, for real, once you left the crew."

"Yeah? I gave up drinking."

"For real?"

"For real," Cady says, then we sit there in silence. We feel the four years between us like a punching bag, waiting for someone to brace it so the other can start swinging. She looks so different now. Longer hair, make-up, a smile.

"So," I say, "you work in a café."

"No. I own a café. Bought it last year, renovated it myself."

"It's nice," I say.

"It's mine. I'm proud of it."

I nod my head towards the door. "That kid in there—"

"No," Cady says.

"I gotta. I'm here to work."

Cady trots out the old joke. "It's not a job. It's a calling."

"Our calling."

"No." Cady finishes her cigarette. "Not anymore. I got other responsibilities now. Twelve employees who need me to run this place, keep earning money so their paychecks show up the reg."

"That ain't fair," I tell her.

"Ain't no part of what you do is fair. I've made my peace with that."

"It's end of the world shit," I tell her

Cady dumps her cigarette butt into the rusting tin. "It's always end of the world shit," she says. "But the world ain't actually ended. I'll talk to the kid, get him to knock off whatever shit he's doing, but you don't walk in there like a berserker. That shit doesn't touch my life anymore."

I don't tell Wiki—I know how he gets—but I keep tabs on the café. Use the excuse I'm checking on the kid, ensuring he stays straight, but I'm mostly there to watch over Cady. Figure out how we'll get her back.

I gotta admit, Cady knows what she's doing there. Seems like the staff and the regulars all have a little crush on her. Monday nights are open night—god-awful poetry, rough-as-rust comedy, singer-songwriters crooning to songs of varying quality.

Tuesdays and Thursdays, there are meetings in the café's corner tables: one for local ride share drivers looking for form a union, another is a women's group where no male-identifying clientele are allowed through doors.

very night, after the café closes, Cady and a staff member take leftovers to a local shelter, along with two urns of decent coffee.

I keep watch on her for a month, because I don't get what she's doing. On the second full moon, the night after Wiki and I get torn to shit by a couple of werewolves, Cady sneaks up on my perch on a nearby building and puts a long black by my side.

"If you're going to loom like a gargoyle," she says, "you may as well order from time to time."

"Just checking in on the kid," I tell her. "Making sure he ain't summoning nothing that shouldn't be on this plane of existence."

"His name's Jonas," Cady says. "He's seventeen years old, trying to deal with a whole lot of shit going down with his family. His mum's diagnosed with cancer, his father's long gone."

"He summoned the Elohim."

"And now he's knocked it off," she says. "I told you I'd talk to him about it. He made me a promise, and he's kept to it, yeah?"

I don't want to concede the point, so I take a sip of the long black. It's delicious—dark and bitter, takes the edge off the cold wind ripping across the rooftop.

"I don't get it, all of this. How in hell does running a café compare to what we used to fight together?"

"There's worse monsters than werewolves and Chupacabra in this world," Cady says. "Most of them have money, or power over people. Most of them are assholes. The worst are all of the above, and stopping them takes more than throwing a punch. Repairing the damage they do takes even more."

"You make coffee."

"I run a café. I give folks a place to come and hide from the world when they need it." Cady cupped her fingers around a fresh cigarette. Summoned a flame to light it. "I put my money towards bigger problems than whatever shit's hitting the fan this week, 'cause the world ain't been devoured by a demon in our lifetime, but there's plenty of other shit that's gone extraordinarily wrong, my friend."

"I just don't get it," I tell her.

"You will, one day," she says. "Unless the inevitable happens, and one of the nasties makes you dead."

"They ain't got me yet."

"No. But if they ain't got you by next Monday, you should actually come in for open mic. Listen to things up close."

I don't go to the open mic on Monday. I don't watch the café anymore, figure there's going to be a sign if Jonas reneges on his promise to Cady and summons angels once more. Wiki and I go fight a ghoul swarm attempting to tunnel free of the local cemetery, discover they're fleeing some radioactive sludge being dumped on the edge of their territory.

Wiki traces things back to the CEO of a local disposals company, and hatches a plan to turn the ghouls on him. Poetic justice, Wiki says.

Our next job is Chupacabra again, but this time, they're being imported by some jackass smuggler. I take a great deal of pleasure in punching him out once we've taken care of the threat.

It keeps coming, though: Harpies recruited by some pop star to prop up an ailing singer; a bunch of jocks summoning a succubus in the hopes of avoiding Me Too claims. Zombie swarms gathering in abandoned plants, dressed up like soldiers because some general wants to create an unstoppable killing force and just thinks they need to find a way to stop the dead from eating brains.

It gets to you, after a while. Even someone as dim as me figures out there's more than just the monsters here, and we're punching the wrong things.

One year later, on the anniversary of the day I figured out where Cady went, me and Wiki are up on the Hotel roof, flicking pillow mints into an empty tin to keep ourselves from smoking. There are storm clouds brewing, low and dark, and Wiki spares them a withering glance. "Even money says there's an apocalypse brewing. Going to be a busy night."

But it's not like we can just skive off work and stop it. There's rent to be paid on our apartment and the doctor's bills add up in this line of work, so there's another three hours on our shift before the break. Three hours before we can get out there and deal with the latest crisis.

That night, we go out and deal with a warlock trying to bring an old god to earth. He's further along than you'd hope for that kind of job. Three hours buys him plenty of time, which means we're fighting a squid-faced monster four times our size in addition to this guy's magic.

The next morning, I go see my boss and had in my two-week's notice. They offer to let me walk rather than work out my notice period. I don't bother telling Wiki about it. He'd only try to stop me, play on the fact we have a destiny.

But sometimes a calling is best ignored. You don't have to obey the rules laid out, especially when they're stacked against you.

I hie my ass over to the university and walk into Cady's coffee shop. There's a tall, reedy kid working the counter. It's a slow and languid Tuesday, no sign of Cady on the floor.

"Hi," the kid says. "What can I get you?"

"Well," I say, "let's start with a long black. Then I'd like to talk to the manager about submitting an application."

NOS, THE BEETLE SLAYER

The Beetle Slayer tramped into town two hours after sunset, emerging from the Barrows with a sword at his hip and a long-knife in his boot. Small, for a warrior, and wiry rather than sheathed in muscles like our local soldiers, Gorus, Stark, and Knox, who purport to keep the village safe. Too many of us looked upon him, this short man who strode like a rooster through the roost, and wandered who he believed he was fooling.

I was there in the Sparrowhawk when he sidled through the doors, strolling towards the bar like a triumphant hero, the Barrow's dust still clinging to his boots. He flashed the barman, Old Eustace, a wide grin, and ordered a tankard of ale.

It was Gorus who made the first move, removing his paw from Callie Amberwine's ass and crossing the taproom to loom over the newcomer. Gorus made a show of his well-met-stranger, and-who-might-you-be routine, but there was no mistaking the way he held himself straight and tall, nor the way he crossed the battle-scarred arms to show off the legacy of his prowess.

We all held our breath, for we knew this routine. Had seen it play out, time and again, since we'd made the mistake of hiring Gorus to protect our village from bandits three winters past and realized they would never leave.

But the small newcomer cared not for scars or height, nor the breath held by every villager sitting there to watch the exchange.

"You can call me Nos," he said. "The Beetle Slayer, late of the Karthadine Coast. Pleasure to make your acquaintance."

"Well, Beetle Slayer, I'm Gorus of the Red Tier. Over there are Stark and Knox, the brothers of the Axe. They have hired us to keep this town safe, and we want no trouble out of the likes of you."

Nos tipped his cap at all three men, then collected his tankard and drank deep. "My dear Gorus, I would not dream of doing more than enjoying an ale and kick off the gust of the road for an evening. You have naught to concern yourself with me, unless you've got beetles that need slaying."

Gorus exchanged a look with the brothers, and they nodded their satisfaction. Tension eased as our valiant guardsmen assumed the stranger knew his place, and knew not to tarry here, lest their villainy be discovered.

Those of us who hoped the tiny rooster may be up to the fight, a potential savior, quietly packed our hopes and tucked them away once more, resigned to the inevitable.

In theory, Nos The Beetle Slayer paid for a spot in the common room of the Tavern, but there's no evidence he camped there after paying his coin to Old Eustace for the right. Last anyone remembers, he announced his fourth tankard a potent drop and excused himself to use the privy, and in the bustle of the late evening nobody noticed he did not return. A stranger—even one so visible as Nos—meant little in our town these days, for Gorus and the Brothers would move them on before morning and things would be as they had been ever since the trio arrived.

Last drinks were called, and the trio wound down for the night, Gorus heading for the private room at the back at the tavern, Knox returning to the Widow Hasther's hut down by the river, and Stark electing to go to the old guard house that ostensibly served as the warrior's home. We knew how things would go from there and kept our tongues stilled lest things go worse.

It wasn't long after the entire village roused to the Widow Hasther's screams, and discovered the barrel-chested, red-bearded Knox had been stabbed three times while he lay in his bed. We all gathered, drawn by the noise, and observed the crimson sheets and the foul air of Knox's voided bowels at the time of death. Some of us thrilled at the notion three had become two, but that hope proved short-lived as Gorus and Stark realized their comrade was dead. At first, they blamed the Widow Hasther, assuming he'd pushed the widow past her limit and she'd after Knox with a carving knife.

Then they remembered Nos, and the wicket long-knife in his boot. It also occurred to them Nos wasn't among the crowd who'd gathered around the Widow's hut.

Even a brute like Gorus can put two and two together, when they realize there's a threat, and they broke apart to search for the stranger and get a measure of revenge.

Smarter men would have worked together, staying close rather than splitting their forces, but Gorus and Stark felt the confidence of large, muscled men hunting down smaller prey. Gorus drew his sword and went left, heading for the outer wall of the village, while Stark held his axe in a two-handed grip and commandeered three of the local men to help search the river shore. They were not smart men, for all their cruel cunning, and Stark soon paid the price for it.

One fisher he'd pressed into service noticed a small boat missing from the shore, and Start demanded they got out after Nos despite the dangers of being on the water after dark. The fishers hemmed and hawed, making it clear it was no sound plan, but Stark thumbed his axe and leveled a baleful glance, and soon they were shoving the boat off the shore and climbing aboard in the lantern light.

To hear Old Mett, the fisher, tell it, Nos came up on them in the dark, swimming through the dark waters of the river with a blade in his teeth. He slithered over the side, quick as an eel, and sliced the blade across Stark's heels, toppling the big man over and into the water, where the current pulled him under and swept him downriver towards the sea.

"What else could I do?" Old Mett asked plaintively, repeating the story for an angry Gorus. "I'm an old man, and I can't haul a man like Stark to shore. And we pay *you to* hold off brutes and swordsman like this Beetle Slayer."

Gorus damned Old Mett's eyes and threw him to the ground, swearing that Nos the Beetle Slayer would die before the night was out. He gathered us all, man, woman, and child, and demanded we search house to house. Nobody would engage the small man, but they'd raise a cry when he was discovered.

"I'll crush this interloper like the bug he is," Gorus said. "All you need to do is find him."

For a man like Nos to succeed as a warrior, he must be fast and good rather than strong. He must pick his moments and prick his opponent, find the weak spots in his armor, rather than crash through his defenses and batter away with raw power.

When the cry went up that Nos had been found, and we sent Gorus into Hannie Miller's barn to take care of the interloper, we assumed the strength and armor of Gorus would make all the difference. But when the hullabaloo of the quick battle was over, and we all ventured in to observe the aftermath, we discovered a dozen grievous wounds had pricked Gorus' corpse. Here, sharp jabs with a bladed weapon, three precise stabs in a row. There, shallow cuts that bled the man and left him weakened. On his neck, the red mark of rope burn where Nos caught him in a tight noose and strangled him before launching the rapid assault.

Gorus died an ugly, bloody death, gasping for oxygen.

This is the tale we tell people when they ask what happened to Gorus and Knox and Stark, our brave protectors. Nos the Beetle Slayer came, and he proved too much for the trio.

In the parts of the tale we don't tell, I was the one who encountered Nos the following morning, when he emerged mole-eyed and yawning from my father's barn. A small, wiry man who'd slept well that night, the road dust replaced by straw and splashes of mud where he's walked past the pig trough.

He apologized to me and offered a coin in recompense for his lodging. "I thought it best not to stay where your towns guard could find me," he said. "No offense, but they seem like a nasty crew."

"They were," I said. "But they're dead now."

"Dead?" Nos the Beetle Slayer raised his eyebrows and dropped one hand to the sword at his waist. "Were you attacked in the night?"

"In a way," I told him. "A swordsman came to town, and they didn't like the look of him. Thought they might do something untoward, only to discover the stranger was wily and led them on a merry chase. He picked them off one by one, a feat of arms they could well write songs about."

Nos gaped at me like a carp. "Your stranger had a busy night."

"He did. He should also move on," I said, "before someone comes looking for Gorus or Knox or Stark. It would not do to be here, in town, where anyone might find them."

We stared at one another for a long time. Nos broke away first, his gaze dropping to the coin he'd offered me for the night in our barn. He very quietly returned it to his purse, and puffed his chest out in false bravado.

"If they were nasty folk," he said, "a swordsman might be forgiven for wondering if there were a reward for their deaths. Something to make up for the trouble of watching his back for vengeful brothers."

"There might be," I said. "Although any strangers who asked questions would be warned away. The swordsman was quite lethal, and studiously wiped all three out in the space of a single night."

Nos chewed that over, hand on his sword hilt, and finally broke into a grin.

"Well," he said. "Seems your swordsman was a dab hand at slaying more than giant beetles, in the end."

We shook on it, and I gave him the small sack of coin we'd gathered tighter. Not much, but enough to send him off with a spring in his step and a smile on his lips.

And the town, well, we said nothing of it. That Nos the Beetle Slayer had come in and unleashed such carnage was agreed upon and repeated until it became truth, and it's a story we've had to repeat once or twice in the years since.

Nos, the Beetle Slayer. A small man, but deadly, and our savior.

INFECTION VECTORS

Gill kneels beside the corpse, poking at the shattered remains of the skull with the point of his pocket knife. The dead man's one of the Scarecrow Dandys—top hat, tails, Hessian sack for a mask—but his death has made a mess of that, the mask ripped open and the tailored jacket torn. What's left of his brains resembles pâté left too long in the sun.

He's one of the boys from Montague Road, a long way from home.

"Marion's going to be pissed," Gill says.

Amanda's shadow falls across the dead man's face and she scuffs her sneaker against the concrete. "Spider Marion's always pissed." Her breath steams in the frosty morning air as she speaks. "Unless he comes down past Turin Street, no-one's going to care."

Gill slips gloves on and examines the knife, frowning at the verdant tinge when the light hits the gray-matter smeared on the tip. Rubs his cheek with his free hand.

"Crap," he says, quietly, and Amanda crouches down beside him. She squints at the tinge, slender fingers resting against his shoulder, and agrees with his assessment in the same low whisper. The green tinge is a sign of viral infection, triggering secondary mutations among the gene-spliced and the engineered. Corporate work, not something naturally occurring.

Not such a big deal cityside, but out here where the gangs rewrite their genes like changing clothes, it could be catastrophic. "We'll need to track the infection," he said. "If it's wide-ranging, corporate will need to report it. Get the whole district quarantined. If not, we extract patient zero and hand them over to the lab boys, yeah?"

Amanda presses against Gill's shoulder and stands, gazing toward the mouth of the alley. She unsheathes the knife at the small of her back, a combat weapon sharper and longer than Gill's puny blade. His knife is a tool. Her knife's made for gutting people and pulling out their gizzards.

"So much for an easy clean-up," Amanda says. "I guess we're going hunting."

Gill nods, still frowning, and gets to his feet. It's going to be a long, long night.

Mother Kong hammers Amanda in the mouth, knocks her to the floor in a spray of sweat and blood. Her knife tumbles free of her fingers and skitters across the concrete, comes to rest against the red brick wall just beyond her reach. Mother roars and slams both fists against Amanda's back, drops all four hundred pounds of genetically spliced muscle against his partner's spine.

It astounds him Amanda's still moving after. That she isn't broken in half.

Gill lunges for the knife, blood pulsing against his temples. He doesn't want it—the average member of The Rampage starts off at six-three, big before they splice their genes with custom DNA from rhinos, gorillas, and crocodiles. Picking a fight with one of The Rampage is like messing with kaiju that's done a line of ketamine, and hand-to-hand has never been Gill's strength.

But letting Amanda get torn apart isn't good news either, so Gill picks up the knife and ducks when Mother takes a swing at him, feels shards of brick in his hair as the wall cracks under the impact. Gill stabs and the blade skitters across Mother's scales.

Useless. Mother Kong rounds on him, nostrils flared, and Gill prepares to die.

Then Amanda twists free of the big woman's weight, scrambling to her feet. Kong stands, uncertain, and Amanda seizes the moment, smashing a kick into a trunk-like knee with the force to damage cartilage. Mother Kong staggers and Amanda levers her to the floor, grabs the leg and bends the joint in a direction it's never meant to go.

Gill blinks, surprised by his partner's strength. She's always been faster, always better, but never like this.

"Knife," Amanda barks, and jars him out of the reverie. Gill throws it to her underhand. Holds his breath as she snatches it from the air and jams the blade into the ligaments. Mother makes a strangled noise, head arcing back in agony. She offers Gill a blood-stained grin and says, "Go ahead. Ask."

Gill nods and clicks his fingers in front of Mother's face. "Kong," he says. "Hey, Kong. Time for quiet now, eh?"

He waits. The pained snarls become a whimper. Kong accepts she's beaten.

"There's a dead guy on your patch," Gill says. He produces the slide from his pocket, holds it to the light. "Looks like a chimera got him, infected him with something nasty."

Mother snarls, lips peeling back from canines that resemble rusty nails.

"It was one of your boys who crushed the guy's skull Kong. We just wanna know if he's infected or the infected." Gill gets out his pocket knife, unfolds the blade. He places the point in the corner of Mother's right eye. "Don't think I won't go digging for information, if that's what it takes."

Mother doesn't show fear, but her black pupils flick toward the knife.

"Infectee," she says. "He got bit in a rumble with the rat boys last week." She blinks very carefully, conscious of the blade. "I can give you a name..."

. . .

Amanda grabs Scabbie by the collar of his flannel shirt, rams him against the concrete pylon. Gill holds a handkerchief against his nose, trying to block the fetid smell of too many bodies in an enclosed space. The rat boys nest in an abandoned car park down by Red Square, barricading the entrance with rusting wrecks and heaped piles of trash. Gill casts a glance at the shadows corners, wary of skittering claws against the concrete floor. Amanda plants a knee in her Scabbie's crotch, just to make it clear what's coming.

"We need a name, man," Amanda says. "One of yours infected a rampage with a strain of chimera virus, and nobody wants that shit spreading and mucking up their DNA."

Scabbie's head lolls to the side. He's already half-blind in his left eye, courtesy of the bruises and oozing blood. Narrow fingers scrabble against Amanda's jacket, trying to dislodge her grip. Gill just waits, all nervous, arms folded. No use making threats here, not unless you back 'em up. He can bluff the Rampage 'cause the Rampage like to fight, but Rat Boys join up 'cause they believe in the cause. There's no reason to live down there otherwise, in the dirt and decaying trash. "Pink-skins," Scabbie hisses. "Servants of the dollar."

"We're talking about a chimera, scabs. That's a danger to your crew as much as all the others." She pushes closer and Scabbie looks away, his whiskers brushing against her cheek. "Don't be stupid, Scabbie. We're not looking to cause you problems—we're just cleaning up a mess."

Scabbie's hiss comes from somewhere deep in the back of his throat.

Gill puts his hand on Amanda's shoulder, pulls her back a little. "Last count said there were fifty-two people wearing rat boy colors," he says. "There's thirty-three Rampage, give or take. Three times as many Crow boys than both your crews combined, and they've been hitting the 'morphs way harder than any of you. What do you think happens if the virus hits those guys, Scabs? What happens to your little crew of anarchists when the Corvidae mutate and go mad?"

Scabbie glares at Gill, his snarl dying away.

"Dresden," he says. "Her name is Liesel Dresden. But she shouldn't have been infected, brah. She wasn't one of us." His nose twitches as he looks from Gill to Amanda and back again, desperation in his eyes. "She was one of Toby Cog's freaks—no gene-morph's required."

It's dark inside the clock tower and the air tastes of dust and oil and steel. "It's not that I'm unsympathetic to their cause," Cog says, tugging back a crimson cloak to expose his clockwork arm. "The human form was never meant to remain inviolate, not given what we know and what we could become. I simply disagree with their methods and their obsession soft and worthless flesh." He tilts his handsome face to the left in a curt, mechanical gesture. One eye is a circle of dark green glass welded to the socket with a plate of burnished copper. His other eye is human, its pupil the size of pins prick. Gill sags in the grip of Cog's lieutenant, aware that he'll suffer if he looks away.

"The great flaw of gene-splicing has always been its uncertainty," Cog says. "The hope that one's mutations will somehow be beneficial. My brothers have always been the cast-offs, the unwanted results when initiations go wrong."

The flunky drags Gill to the edge of the platform, holds him over the railing to look down at the long drop into the tower's twitching gears. Gill catches a flash of movement—Amanda clinging to a rusting ladder, reaching for the struts that support the underside of platform. Still alive after being tossed over the edge. All Gill needs to do is play for time, let her get into position.

"So tell me, Mister Gill, is what I do so wrong?" Cog says. "I take those affected by uncertainty and deliver the assurance of pure, unaltered steel. I give them the promise that everything will be as they expected, rather than faint hopes."

"It's not wrong, but it's stupid." Gill says. "Liesel Dresden isn't mutant, she's *mutating*. A work I progress."

Cog hisses. He doesn't enjoy interruptions. Gill closes his eyes so he doesn't have to watch the end coming. "You can't just slap a new arm on her or replace the left side of her skull," he says. "She's infected, Toby. She's dangerous."

"Not to me," Cog says. "Not to any of mine."

"All of yours started out with other crews. A lot of them were gene-spliced."

"But I fixed them," Toby Cog says, and he titters like a man whose sanity is dancing along a high wire. "I fixed them and showed them a way."

"Honestly, Cog, you just made a mess." The platform lists as Amanda hauls herself over the railings. There's a gash on her forehead and a bruise on her arm, but there's something cold and certain in her eyes as she stares Cog down. "Now hand over Gill and give me a location."

"Never!" Cog charges in a swirl of cape and clanging feet. He swings his heavy cane at Amanda's head, looks surprised when she ducks the blow and uses his own momentum. Gill watches the cyborg twist in the air, desperately snagging the rail with his fleshy hand. He hangs there, too heavy to haul himself up, as Amanda draws her knife and taps it against the rail.

"It's a long way down, Cog," she says. "Far enough that even you'll dent when you hit the ground. We need Liesel Dresden, and you're going to give her over…"

They find Liesel Dresden holed up in an old McDonalds, hiding behind the rusting deep fryers. Spines where her hair should be, huge tusks jutting from her jaw. Her right forearm is covered in ark feathers that gleam like oil on concrete..

She's hostile, but there's no choice in that. The virus has her in its grip. Gill lets Amanda handle the violence, comes in once Dresden is subdued and shackled. He makes an incision in the side of her neck with a pocket knife. Green puss seeps out before the first drop of blood.

"Christ," Amanda says. "That's almost bloody beautiful."

Gill scowls and folds his knife shut. "Pity you didn't kill her. It would have been a mercy."

"Orders were to capture," Amanda says.

"Sure," Gill says. "Orders." He takes a blood sample and wipes it against a glass tile, seals that in a plastic bag. "Corporate got a head-count on how many she's killed?"

"Six," Amanda says. "Maybe seven."

"Such a bloody waste." Gill pockets the sample and wipes both hands against his grubby jeans. He can't see the beauty Amanda sees, not in this patchwork mess that used to be a human being. "Tag her and call the corporate in. Get her into a lab so they can get started on the new strain."

"The new strain?" The surprise in her voice makes Gill wary. He turns and retreats a step when he meets Amanda's stare.

"Amanda," he says, but there's no question in it. The thing wearing Amanda's face advances, big knife in her grip. Her skin ripples when she moves, reshapes itself from pale skin to something dark and rough. "They don't want a new strain, Gill. I think they've got it right."

The knife lashes out and he stumbles back, scrambling to put space between them.

"They spliced me before they sent me into the field." It's not Amanda's voice anymore, pitched so low and guttural. "I got a whole grab-bag of traits they wanted: strength; speed; instincts. An enhanced sense of smell. They wanted to make sure that I could handle things if we ever got in trouble."

Gill's mouth goes dry. He runs through his short list of potential weapons: a pocket knife; a handkerchief; five hundred in cash and his access to corporate credit. None of them feasible against the thing peeling itself free of his former partner's skin.

"So tell me, Gill," she says. "What did they splice you for before they deployed you."

Gill backs into a wall. "Nothing," he says. They didn't bother. I'm still... my genes are clean."

"Pity." Amanda's smile belongs to a predator. She steps closer, looming over him. Her mouth is full of small, sharp teeth.

"Waste not, want not, then," she says. "Phase two was always meant to be a test of whether we could induce mutation in a clean-gene, and you weren't the *worst* partner they've paired me with…"

ON THE CORNER OF CAXTON AND PETRIE, 12:04 AM

Heathcliff Carter stumbled out of the Caxton's front bar three sheets to the wind. The warm Brisbane summer night embraced him like an old friend, and he caught the scent of roasting schnitzel at the Windmill Cafe on the corner. His stomach rumbled, a loud reminder that he'd consumed nothing but Heineken, salt, lemon, and shots of Cuervo for the last eight hours. Time to eat, he figured, and lurched his way across the bustling street.

He was halfway through a schnitty burger with the lot when the portal manifested, a shimmering sphere of blue-white light bursting into existence in the heart of the Petrie Terrace intersection. The late-night traffic veered around it, careening through the busy intersection and crashing into the Barracks' walls. A four-wheel drive with a soccer-mom behind the wheel hammered into the streetlight just out front. Screams, curses, and car horns punctuated the muggy night.

The first invader strode through the portal with purpose, a strapping Viking with an axe and red hair pulled into tight war-braids. Red Braid roared a battle cry and charged the nearest cluster of civilians, the rest of his war-band spewing forth to back-up their war leader. The two cops who'd been working the strip both went for their guns, opening fire in a futile attempt to stem the tide.

One raider smashed through the glass door of the Windmill. Heathcliff sighed and put down his burger. He really wasn't sober enough to deal with temporal disruption tonight.

"Oi, mate," he said. "Enough of that. Pack it in and hie your ass back to your own neck of space and time."

The raider whirled and fixed Heathcliff with a wild-eyed, berserker stare. Heathcliff huffed his annoyance and clambered out of his seat, wiping burger grease off his hands with a napkin.

The Viking charged and Heathcliff ducked under the wild swing, used the momentum to flip his attacker up and over, then through the Formica table covered in his half-eaten dinner. The Viking sprawled amid the wreckage, the remnants of Heathcliff's burger clinging to a scar-covered forehead, groggy and rattled.

Heathcliff laid claim to the Viking's sword and dragged the big man by the war braids, lurching his way out into the unleashed carnage on Petrie Terrace. Security from the pubs and clubs were doing their best to help the cops, but the Vikings outnumbered them and a screaming mob of drunk, terrified revelers trying to escape the war raid weren't helping things. The portal hummed at full power, maintaining integrity far longer than any naturally occurring rift in space-time ever would. Heathcliff dropped his Viking and clambered onto the roof of the crashed four-wheel drive, surveyed everything with a steely bravado he hoped would hide exactly how much he'd drunk.

He dredged his brain for some ancient Norwegian, but without a temporal service translator, he had to rely on basic phrases learned in his rookie year. Best not to attempt them. Volume and tone could bridge the gap.

"ALRIGHT," he bellowed, waving his blade. "EVERY SINGLE ONE OF YOUR VIKING MOTHERFUCKERS CAN STOWE YOUR ROLL RIGHT FUCKING NOW."

Volume and irritation did the job. Two dozen Viking eyes turned towards him, as did the cops, the security guards, and the vast majority of the panicked crowd trying to escape. One raider charged Heathcliff's position, and Heathcliff showed him the error of his ways with a swift kick to the face.

Twenty-three of them to go.

Heathcliff pointed at the leader, the big redhead with braids who'd led the charge. "You, fuckhead, I know this wasn't your idea. Someone's playing you and your mob for a patsy, and you've got this one chance to pack your shit up and go back to your own space-time before shit gets nasty."

The Viking thumped his chest and pointed the battle-axe in Heathcliff's direction. A bellowed war cry followed, quickly taken up by the rest of the band, all of them thumping their chest and shouting to the gods in resonant baritones. Heathcliff couldn't make out much with his limited vocabulary in their native tongue, but he recognized the name of several gods and figured it for a battle-prayer.

Stupid fucking Vikings. Always doing things the hard way.

At least Heathcliff held the higher ground.

Heathcliff brought the blade up, ready to repel the first attacker. He figured he was good for at least the first five, even if they charged en masse; might even hold off a good dozen if he was fighting sober. Drunk and caught off-guard, he'd be fighting for time instead. Hoping the authorities could scramble a team to contain the situation before the casualties piled up and added them to the numbers.

"Bring it on, assholes," he barked, and the Vikings swarmed. The first swung a sword at Heathcliff's knee, overextended and fell against the car when Heathcliff parried the blade. The second swung a battle-axe in a slow, vicious arc, and Heathcliff leapt over the scything strike with ease. He retaliated with kicks and strikes, sprays of blood arcing through the night air, doing his best to hold on and stay breathing.

The war leader didn't join the charge. The big redhead held back, assessing with cold eyes, leaving it to the rest of the band to wear Heathcliff down. Smarter than he looked, although the Vikings often were. Half the reason they were in the top ten threats to breach the temporal barrier.

A cop joined in, opening fire on the attackers crowded around the four-wheel drive. The leader squinted, stitching together the cause-and-effect as an unfamiliar weapon mowed down his men. A vicious grin broke out beneath the bushy beard. Red Braid was smarter than he looked and determined to eliminate the threat.

Heathcliff screamed a warning, threw his blade at the big Viking. It caught Red Braid in the shoulder, biting through flesh. Sufficient to return the big man's attention to Heathcliff, and give the cop a little time to second-guess getting involved in the fracas.

Of course, Heathcliff was weaponless now, and there were still sixteen angry Vikings cutting off any escape from the car's roof.

He almost breathed a sigh of relief when Agent Kulp finally stepped through one of the Agency's smaller, controlled temporal rifts and flashed the scene to stow chronological time to a screeching halt. Cops, crowd, and Vikings froze in place.

Heathcliff noted his exact position, in case they needed to restart, then collapsed with a sigh of relief.

"Took your fucking time, mate," he said. "These assholes have been active in the time stream for ten minutes."

Kulp ignored him, making a beeline for the roiling portal that gave them access. "Expected you could handle them," she said. "Well-trained agent on the scene and all that."

"It's my night off," Heathcliff said. "And my gear's back in the office."

Kulp shook her head. "A good agent's always prepared, my friend."

Heathcliff rolled his eyes. "Just promise we've got this one contained. I like this timeline."

"We can contain it," Kulp said. "Body count isn't too high, thanks to your work, and the edit team is preparing cover stories as we speak. The only problem is this bad-boy." She crouched and produced a pencil from the depths of her blazer, delivering an experimental poke to the to portal. It flickered at the contact, and Kulp bit her lower lip.

Heathcliff's stomach rumbled. Stepping into a temporal bubble always burned off calories faster than living in a chronological progression.

"Figure that's your problem to solve," he said. "I've still gotta rustle up some grub and sleep off a vicious hangover. You right to handle all this?"

"Everything except the paperwork."

Heathcliff shook his head. Always the fucking paperwork, but at least he didn't have to re-enter the time-stream in mid-brawl again.

"I'll get to it on Monday, whenever I make it to the new week. Give me a twenty-count to get some distance, then blip me out so I can get on with my evening, yeah?"

Kulp waved him off, already too deep into the investigation. The other agents contained the scene, but Kulp would tackle the mysteries: how had the Vikings accessed portal technology? What led them to this part of space/time? Heathcliff re-tucked his shirt and picked a direction, heading back towards the city. The twenty-four-hour Hungry Jacks in the mall wasn't anywhere near as good as the Windmill's schnittys, but the agency would keep the corner of Caxton and Petrie tied up for hours while they investigated.

Plus, from there he could catch a train home. Doze for a few hours, ease through the hangover, and let the adrenaline wear down.

If Heathcliff got lucky, Kulp's investigation would source the creator of the Vikings portal came from. Those details would tell them when and where the culprit existed, how the agency could track them down.

Heathcliff looked forward to exchanging stern words about interrupting a man's night off.

But that was tomorrow's problem, whenever tomorrow arrived.

A GOOD THEIF'S CHOICES

Malachi pressed close to the ivory door, taut as a cat skulking through a dog-filled alley. He'd crept his way to this chamber, wide and domed with verdigris stone, the rough flagstones on the floor slick with some liquid he couldn't identify. A stone plinth sat in the center of the room, and upon it a glistening black pearl the size of a large man's fist. Four braziers sat on golden tripods, spewing heady smoke into the air, but there was no sign of a guard or warding runes that Malachi could detect.

Trapped, then, he decided. Only thing that made sense. He steeled himself and ventured into the chamber, moving slow and light. With every step he stopped and listened, waiting for the telltale snick indicating he'd placed a foot upon a flagstone which activated a trap, but the floor proved safe. It made no sense: rumor had it the Horrormancer's Pearl was among the most secure treasures in Bok-Rezel, but aside from the red-eyed, listless guards on the upper levels of the tower, he'd encountered nothing more complex than pin-and-tumbler locks. If no great defense manifested itself here, in the very chamber that housed the treasure, then making off with the pearl would prove a doddle and his life would fall into place. Finn Colough would pay handsomely for the score, leaving Malachi with twenty bags of gold, and that gold would secure Ben Oberon's hand, even if his parents objected to Malachi's suite.

"The things we do for love." Malachi shook off the thoughts about what might be and focused on the here and now. Mid-theft was no time to dwell on Ben's tawny hair or lopsided smile, and thieves who let their attention wander were thieves who ended up dead. Nobody married a corpse, even in a city as permissive as Bok-Rezel, no matter how much they loved the man he'd been when he still drew breath.

Focus, then. Assess the threat. The pearl sat, plump and maleficent, on a green-stone plinth. Larger and crueler than a whipped dog. Malachi focused his efforts on the braziers, searching for tripwires strung between the tripods of hallucinogenic magic in the smoke.

Nothing. Mayhap the Horrormancer trusted in his reputation to ward off thieves, or deployed protections more sophisticated than any Malachi knew. Best to assume the latter. A cautious thief lasted far longer than a reckless thief, after all. If they were lucky, they may even marry the man of their dreams.

Malachi crouched low and surveyed the plinth itself, squinting at the dust-choked grooves and decorative carvings. He couldn't detect the telltale tingle of magic, but up close he could make out the faintest curve of script concealed in the design. The sharp cut and whorl of the letters suggested a phrase in the dark tongue, the language handed down from the Dukes and Duchesses of Hell as the world emerged from chaos, but the thick cloak of dust made it impossible to read, although it lacked the telltale silver needed to embed magic in the runes.

Slowly, cautiously, adjusting his balance so he made no contact with the altar, Malachi breathed on the dust to clear it. The pressure—no more than the kiss of a light breeze—brought a sheen of sweat to Malachi's brow, but no ill came from it. Seeing no sign of the warlock's silver in the cut stone, he grew bolder and produced a soft, camel-haired brush from his kit. Three light strokes, no harder than the touch of a landing feather.

Malachi rose to the balls of his feet, stretching out the nerves. He prided himself on keeping a cool head on the job, but the unfamiliar wrongness of a treasure left without defenses put him on edge. He risked a closer look at the pearl itself, the dark shell that roiled and shifted as though smoke were trapped beneath the skin. Malachi's brain rattled off fell curses and unknown defenses that might trigger when it was disturbed, starting with the appearance of a guardian demon and rolling through to some fell death curse that eliminated all life in the tower. His pulse hammered against his skull, loud as a blacksmith's hammer, and for the first time since his apprentice years, Malachi feared he was out of his depth. Faced with a magic he didn't understand, a treasure too dangerous to steal, better to—

He caught the racing thoughts and stepped away from the altar, squaring his shoulders to ease the tension knotting up as the fear took hold. Adrenaline did terrible things to a body, forced mistakes and reckless risks when none were needed. A good thief made friends with the shaky eagerness of fear, but a great one knew to how to clear his mind of what might be and focus on what is. Malachi knew he was a great thief, and it had been years since he'd succumbed to reckless nerves.

A smile blossomed as he recognized the source. He stretched a hand toward the pearl and felt his pulse quicken, the roil of anxiety plaguing his gut as the consequences of failure besieged him.

"Oh, you clever bastard." Leave it to a sorcerer who trade in fear to weaponize a thief's own body as the ultimate defense.

Against a lesser burglar, it might even have been enough, but Malachi prided himself on being a cut above the greatest of the great. He'd honed his body in the mind, trained in petty magics, and knew enough of the greater arcana to recognize and undo most wards. Fear might deter a lesser man, but Malachi worked with his nerves and the threat of disaster for every heist. He welcomed the opportunity to overcome any obstacle.

He forced a smile and crouched low, centered himself with a series of long, slow breaths. Welcomed the fear as a warning of what might happen, but pushed it aside as he focused on the present. There were many threats that might be, but few signs of any defense that might prevent him from lifting the jewel and making his getaway. The pearl would win him gold, and the gold would win him Ben, and the Oberon clan's objections could be damned to the all the hells. Sure, they may never respect him, or offer anything but grudging slightness to their son-in-law, but he'd be with Ben. With Ben! And they could be so happy together.

Of course, Ben loved his family. Their silent scorn would no doubt wear upon him, maybe even seep into the blissful joy of their loving marriage. There was a risk that scorn might fester, allowing Ben to resent Malachi's choices. Whatever thrill there was in loving a thief would surely fade once they were husbands, and a man as handsome and connected as Ben could surely—

"Ah." Malachi reigned in his thoughts and took another step back from the altar. Relief bubbled through him as he recognized the subtlety of the pearl's defenses.

Of course Ben loved him and looked forward to their marriage. He'd kept his profession hidden for the first six months of their courtship, yet Ben accepted it without question once he learned. Only the faintest doubt remained, a legacy of years spent dealing with scoundrels and thieves.

Faint doubt was enough. The Horrormancer's Pearl magnified even the smallest fear. Accreted dark permeations and deadly futures around stray worries, transforming them into nightmares.

The Horrormancer was good. Very good. But Malachi Du Sark was better. His wry laughter echoed off the verdigris stone chamber, and torches flickered as though the whole chamber drew a breath, preparing for his next attempt at the Pearl.

Malachi cleared his mind. He drew in a long, slow breath and focused on the dust in the air. Noted the muggy warmth shed by the flickering torches. On the next breath his attention drifted to the scuff of footsteps on the floor above, a listless guard patrolling, wary of the doorway leading down to the Pearl and the plague of fears it brought forth.

Fear required attention, and Malachi returned his focus to the act of breathing. He reached for the Pearl on reflex, and his fingertips made contact with the skin. His pulse jumped in anticipation, and a new fear took root: what did Finn Colough want from the damnable thing, anyway, to make it worth all those bags of gold?

Malachi prided himself on professionalism, never asking why and merely focusing on what the job demanded, but a magic as potent as the Pearl could devastate in the wrong hands… He imagined Bok-Rezel in the grip of a city-wide fear, but it would not stop there.

With the Pearl, a Magus of greater powers could hold whole nations in the grip of terror. He could plague enemies with nightmares from which they'd never awake.

A man who held the pearl might not need to pay for its acquisition, if he was confident of the control he'd wield once its magics were in hand.

And Finn Colough offered an unseemly amount of gold, more than Malachi had ever heard a good burglar being paid for a job before.

He retrieved his hand and gnawed on a thumbnail, contemplating his approach. Finn Colough had been very clear about the rewards for securing the pearl, with none of the customary threat and bluster if Malachi betrayed him. Such changes in behavior often meant secrets were being kept, and Malachi wandered what Finn had planned. He recognized the Pearl's hands in those thoughts, but it didn't make them any less worthy of consideration.

Malachi settled on his haunches. He'd made no secret of his desire to marry Ben Oberon, and Finn Colough could no doubt play upon that to coax Malachi into taking an ill-advised job with nary a question asked. Malachi exhaled slowly and rubbed his palms together, eying the pearl with open dislike.

Was it prudence, or submission, to walk away at this point?

Malachi placed a hand on the pearl once more. "Show me," he said, welcoming the fear. Ready to see the worst. "What happens if you're removed?"

For a moment, he saw a future where the sky above Bok-Rezel split open and the horrors of the nightmare lands spilled forth as an army. He saw terror stretching across the lands, a black stain seeping through the world like poison through a vein. He saw the return of chaos, humanity crushed beneath its weight, and the end of all things, the entire world flickering out like a candle flame in a storm wind.

He lifted his hand away and retreated three steps. His hand tingled as the pressure abated.

A good thief didn't wait too long to make a decision once it was clear the choice needed to be made.

There were other ways to earn the gold he needed—slower, perhaps, but still achievable. A great thief was never without a score, and Bok-Rezel held plenty of worthy targets for a man of his skills. Malachi stowed his gear and brushed his hands clean, stepping away from the plinth. The dark sheen of the Pearl caught the flickering torchlight, enticing and deadly, but he knew better than to reach for it and trigger a fresh wave of fear.

Malachi dipped his head to the Pearl and retreated. He stole out of the chamber and closed the door, stole his way back to the roof and the slow climb down to freedom. Finn Colough may well send other thieves, but he doubted any sane man or woman would finish the job. Not once they'd seen the consequences of lifting the pearl from its resting place.

He could find another heist to win Ben Oberon's hand. There was always work for a man of his talents, and easier prey he could liberate from its owners with less risk, and that wasn't nothing.

THE CHAP WHO WANTED TO BE COMMANDER FLAG

Yes, I know the rumors. I was there on day one. He lived in a flat below mine, in Spilsby, just near the church of St James. A nice bloke, but a little strange. Into comic books, long before people were into comic books; big fan of Commander Flag before the movies made him well-known.

He'd talked about doing Cosplay before I knew what that was, but took a few years to pull the trigger. So I guess it started slowly, but once it started…well, he moved *fast*.

He sewed his own uniform first. I gather, from our conversations, because the uniform was the easy bit. "Not a lot of mystic ore around, these days, waiting to become a invulnerable shield bequeathed by the spirit of America," he'd say, and then he'd laugh like it was some glorious joke that both of us understood.

I didn't, then, but I liked him. He was better with people than you'd expect. Well liked. *Friendly*.

When the first uniform was a bust, he gathered together some friends who could sew and several meters of red, white and blue fabrics. They cut and measured and shaped for two days, until he the costume down, and while it might not be made of bullet-proof duralumin plates, it did fit and it was comfortable and he rather looked the part if you ignored his spectacles and his stooped frame.

Second, he learned to fight. Boxing, at first, getting the basics of striking and footwork down, but from there a little bit of everything: aikido, karate, sambo, and kickboxing. Four hours of parkour, on the weekends, to keep him fit and flexible.

And while he didn't quite feel like a superhuman soldier blessed by the Spirit of America at the end of it, he stood a little straighter and he looked a whole lot better. Worked away the little pot belly and replaced it with muscle and a fighters instincts.

It took years, but he did it. He was that kind of guy.

The shield proved difficult, because a replica wasn't enough for him. He wanted something serviceable, which meant paying attention to alloys and weight. Stainless steel looked good, but proved too light, and other metals too heavy. In the end, he hired a blacksmith and a metallurgist. Three iterations later, he had a shield he could throw around.

I met his mum, once or twice, 'round this period. Not such a nice woman, but I expect that's why she produced offspring determined to become a costumed hero. She didn't understand him and she wasn't afraid to say so. "Why he's spending his hard-earned money, trying to be like some bloody yank," she said. "Really, it rather eludes me. I thought he'd go into dentistry, much like his father."

"He's not an American hero," her son would argue. "We've all got flags, mum. We're all proud of our country."

"Doesn't matter what he's called," his mum always said. "Man wears the stars and stripes on his uniform, and there's only one flag he's representing. If you think otherwise, you're barmy."

Many of his friends, who I knew from the pub, tended to agree with her. They were chippies and plumbers and cabinet makers, practical kind of men with bills to pay and families that needed feeding.

But after a year of testing – a very long year, in many respects – and more money than he should have spent, the chap who wanted to be Commander Flag went and collected his shield.

The blacksmith had done beautiful work, I'll give him that. Light, it was, and easy to carry, and harder than you'd expect from its layers of candy-reds and blues painted over the white gold. He had them test it for him, the metallurgist and the blacksmith. Had them shoot it with guns up to fifty calibre, to assure himself it was the kind of thing that could truly stop a bullet.

And that evening, once he'd brought the shield home, he put on his uniform and collected the shield and came downstairs to borrow my mirror. His – he only had one, small and cracked, set above his bathroom sink – wasn't quite long enough to get a proper reflection. I had this full-length thing I'd inherited from my aunt. He stood before it, struck a pose.

He'd filled out nicely, thanks to the training. He was stronger than he'd once been, and definitely faster, and with the shield added to the uniform for the very first time, he rather felt that the time and money had been well-spent.

"You're a bloody fool," his mother said, the first time she saw him in the full ensemble, standing there in uniform with his specs perched on his nose and the shield strapped to his arm.

His friends at the pub said much the same, although they used somewhat nastier language for it. He didn't care, not really. For one, he didn't drink much anymore, because of his training. For another...

Well.

We all know how people can be.

This was his thing, he'd worked quite hard to make it happen, and he was proud of what he'd done. But a few weeks went by and he talked about it less, and after a few months he stopped wearing the uniform out in public. He put the shield up on the mantle, above the fireplace, like a trophy. When visitors came round and asked about it, he'd laugh about it.

"Oh that," he'd tell them. "That was present I got for myself, back when I was younger. Purely decorative, don't you know."

We thought that was the end of it, his Commander Flag thing. He did nothing to prove us wrong.

That summer, the aliens invaded.

Ask the English and they'll tell you that London was the first to be hit. One moment it was an ordinary day: grey skies; sodden rain; waiting for the tube. The next moment: spaceships, looming overhead; war-machines with long, whip-like tentacles and brightly-flashing laser beams that set the whole world aflame. They destroyed Big Ben and the British Museum, the Tower and Buckingham Palace.

They set fire to the London Eye, which wasn't an act of war, perhaps, so much as a favor they did for us all, but the rest? That was a tragedy. We watched it all happening, on the telly and on the internet, and newsreaders would stop reading and just stare at the carnage. And maybe London did go first – who am I to say? – but the other great cities fell just as fast: London, and Moscow, and Tokyo; Johannesburg and Sydney and all the places in between.

In America – they hit America particularly hard – city after city was eliminated. Occasionally, we'd fight back, and even more occasionally the act of resistance would prove to be a good idea.

Mostly, we just learned to live in fear, waiting for news that our town was next and it was time to get out of their way.

And the chap who wanted to be Commander Flag, he watched it all play out on the telly, just like everyone else did. He felt fear, because everyone felt fear in those days. The world, as we knew it, had changed.

He took comfort in the same stories the rest of us did. "The flu," we'd think, "the common cold will take care of this for us. No way they can survive in our atmosphere, our diseases."

They did. Their spaceships, their war-machines, the suits they wore inside: all hermitically sealed to keep them safe from our germs. They tore through our armies, kept us in retreat. The fear? The fear got worse. We knew we were doomed, as a species.

Eventually, ten days after London fell, they announced the Spilsby evacuation. Army busses would be there in twenty-four, take only the most essential belongings. And the chap who wanted to be Captain Flag, he stood in his flat and looked around. He had no photo albums – all that was online, these days. No pets to rescue, no houseplants, nothing of value, really.

So he picked up his shield, so light, so strong. Essential enough, he figured. And he went into his bedroom, the tiny one up the back of the flat. Putting on the uniform felt better still. And later, when the busses came through and the army was there to help everyone get out in a timely manner, the chap who wanted to be Commander Flag went downstairs in his full kit and announced he wouldn't be going.

We were all down there, in the street, lined up in an orderly fashion. We all looked at him, posing, at the doorway of the flat. One of the soldiers said: "well, who in hell are you, then?"

"No-one, really," the chap who wanted to be Commander Flag said. "Just some bloke who really wants to help you chaps fight back."

I'll be honest, some of us liked the idea of that. One of the soldiers – I'm pretty sure he was some kind of lieutenant – asked the question, real cautious, "but you don't have any powers, right?"

And yes, you laugh at the idea of it now, but… well, there were aliens, weren't there? No harm in being thorough.

The chap who wanted to be Commander Flag was honest: "no, no powers," he said. "Just me, offering to help. That's all we've really got."

Then he said: "it's not about the powers. It's never been about the powers. Just, you know, one guy, doing his best to make a difference."

He hitched up his shield, high on his forearm, and looked towards the black fugue hanging low over London. "Just tell me how I can be useful?"

There's nothing useful about eager civilians in a war zone, or so the lieutenant said. He told his men to get the lunatic on the damn bus, so we could get all this over and done with.

The chap who wanted to be Commander Flag nodded, just like he understood and accepted his lot. Then he turned and ran, Ten years of weekend parkour paid off—he went at a wall, and then he was up and over, neat and pretty as anything.

We didn't see him again, after that. He was gone. But occasionally you'll hear stories, round about the place: chap shows up, with a shield, all red, white, and blue, lending a hand and ambushing aliens, giving folks a chance to run; hooking newcomers up with the resistance, although folks always shy away from admitting that, when the first show up. The stories need to be coaxed out of them, over time, in the quiet bits when we're not fighting or running for our lives.

You have to get to know them, before the questions start. But then, once they trust you: how'd you find us? Who inspired you to join? How'd you get hooked up with our camp?

And often, more often than you'd think, they get this weird look in their eyes. "Well," they'll say, real slow. "Well, look, I know it sounds crazy, but I swear this is true…"

And then they'll tell you a story, hand to God, about the Commander. Still fighting, still carrying a beat-up shield, still doing everything he can to live up to the uniform he wears into battle.

Some folks think he snapped, from the stress, but I don't think that's true. If he's crazy, it's 'cause the world is crazy. He just got there sooner.

And these days, better a hero like him, than having no heroes at all.

ONE LAST JOB, AND THEN SLEEP

"Master Dickerhoof isn't home at present," the butler said, "but if you'd care to leave a card—"

Murdoch pushed in before the old boy blocked the path. "If it's all the same with you, partner, I'll wait until he's free."

"Sir, I'm afraid—"

"Sir is my pappy's name, son, and he was a right son of a bitch." Murdoch lifted his duster, exposing the Pinkerton badge pinned to his vest. The butler's lips stitched up like a seamstress repairing a tear.

Murdoch flashed him a smile to put him at ease, and it seemed to do the opposite. In this, at least, the Butler could well prove smarter than his genius-driven master.

"Name's Sam Murdoch, and I'd take it as a kindness if you went out back and interrupt Old Man Dickerhoof's tinkering." Murdoch let the duster drop, shifted the same hand over to the leather satchel under the other arm. The butler's eyes followed. "We've got important business to discuss, and I followed a long trail to find my way here."

The butler's eyes shifted and swept over Murdoch, taking in the battered hat and grubby duster, the pearl-handled six-irons and trail-worn boots. The old boy sniffed and held out a hand for Murdoch's hat and coat. "If you'd care to take a seat, Master Murdoch, it might be a lengthy wait."

"I got time." Murdoch surrendered his outer layers, but the butler lingered. The old boy coughed politely and nodded at the satchel and gun-belt.

Murdoch shook his head. "Tell Dickerhoof he'll want what I've got with me bad enough to forgive any offense I'll cause," he said. "An' I'd be obliged if you could bring me a coffee while I wait."

He settled into the overstuffed couch and hooked a heel on the low coffee table. Arranged the satchel under one hand and fixed the butler with another smile.

The old boy swept out, spry for his years. Murdoch's amiable expression disappeared the moment the old boy left, replaced by the shrewd stare of a man eager to assess the lay of the land. The parlor contained just two large couches, a wobbly coffee table, and threadbare curtains no longer suited to fending off the afternoon light. Three locks secured the parlor door, brass contraptions more ornate than any mechanism Murdoch had seen in ten years working Special Projects with the Pinkerton Detective Agency.

A faint ozone scent threaded its way up from the floorboards, with a danker, nastier smell beneath, and the hair on Murdoch's arm stood to attention without visible cause.

Bad things happened in Dickerhoof House. Murdoch had no doubts on that. A faint, high-pitched whine registered, and Murdoch struggled to determine whether it was merely distant or fighting its way towards the audible range where human ears caught on.

The butler reappeared with the coffeepot, then disappeared without a word. Murdoch poured a cup and settled in to wait. The coffee wasn't bad, a blessed distraction from the sub-audible hum reverberating through the manor. When he finished the first, there was naught to do but start himself another and wait.

Murdoch had just poured a third cup when Edgar Dickerhoof appeared, limping in from the hall on an ornate cane tipped with quartz and copper. Wild haired, with wire-framed glasses, a grease smudge on his right cheek and bloodstains on the leather apron he wore over a smart suit. Murdoch figured the doctor had come straight from the lab, and clearly he didn't relish interruptions in any form. Shrewd eyes swept down to the satchel tucked at Murdoch's side, weighed it against the boot heel on the coffee table. Murdoch schooled his features, feigning the disinterest of a man here to collect money and no more. Jobs went wrong at this stage, when an agent tipped their hand. Men like Dickerhoof danced the line between insight and obliviousness, and suspicion came as natural as curiosity.

After a moment, Dickerhoof's curiosity won out. "Mister Murdoch, I take it your agency found what I need?"

"Most like," Murdoch said, a bald-faced lie. He knew exactly what he carried. "I can't rightly imagine why anyone would need it, let alone sanction its presence in their home."

Dickerhoof eyed the satchel. A pink, eager tongue darted out to wet thin lips. "I believe what I want is my business, Mister Murdoch. I tasked the agency with acquisition and delivery."

"And the elimination of the man who had it," Murdoch said. "On that, the jobs half done."

"Halide escaped you?"

"He did," Murdoch said. "For now."

"I thought your kind never slept. Isn't that the motto?"

"It is," Murdoch said. "Printed right there on my badge. But doesn't mean a man don't get tired, from time to time."

Dickerhoof's brows dropped and he fingered a button on his cane. Murdoch recognized the subtle threat—men like Dickerhoof didn't use guns, and the genius driving them to madness rode side-by-side with irrational anger.

You could use that to keep 'em off-guard, if you played it right, but it wasn't without risk.

"Ain't like I plan to leave him running around," Murdock said. "Just figured you'd want this pronto, 'specially since acquisition took out Halide's lab and plenty of his men."

Murdoch unfurled the satchel, dug around for the canvas-wrapped cargo within. He passed it to the old man with gentle hands, all too cognizant of the value Dickerhoof placed on the object within. "If you want Halide in a pine box, I'll get started once you confirm we recovered the right cargo. Figured she'd be the more important of the two."

Dickerhoof placed the package on the coffee table and unwrapped it with shaky fingers. Murdoch looked away. He'd seen the canisters filled with viscous liquid too many times already, and had no desire to lay eyes upon the disembodied brain within. Dickerhoof caressed the brass casing, giggling. "Yes," he said. "Oh, yes, Mister Murdoch. You've delivered exactly what I need... for now."

Murdoch exhaled, one obstacle down. Any time you delivered the cargo, without getting blasted to bits, it put you one step closer to closing the case, all clean and tidy like. He braced himself for phase two. "Ain't got no guarantee it's your daughter, of course. Halide kept the gray matter alive, but he hadn't figured out how to let the brain speak. Odds are, it's the right one, but I've only got an inside man's promise Halide preserved your daughter. Logic says it's her. I couldn't find other specimens before his dirigible lab caught fire."

"It's Lucy," Dickerhoof said with beatific confidence. "Nero possessed a sub-par intellect, but a loyal streak ran through him. He'd sworn to keep Lucy alive, after she contracted typhoid out west, and his pride wouldn't accept his failure. If he'd brought her home, consulted with me, there'd be no need to resort to all this. I could have saved her, Mister Murdoch. My resources outstripped Nero Halide's, and my research is undeniable. But this—" Dickerhoof caressed the canister "—this is the hubris of a student who thought himself the master's equal, and it's a mistake I shall correct now you've brought my Lucy home."

Murdoch affected a bland expression to keep disgust at bay. "What you do with the specimen after delivery is up to you," he said. "But the agency would rightly like to make sure I've done right, before we take the other half of my fee."

Dickerhoof's eyes screwed tight with suspicion, and he

twisted the quart-tipped cane between two fingers. This, too, represented the moment where many agents failed, and Murdoch took pains to ensure he didn't resemble a threat. For a moment, Dickerhoof's resolved trembled on a razor's edge, and Murdoch knew money no longer held much value for the Doctor and his genius. He cleared his throat, delivered a quick goad. "Sir, you'll understand we just want to do right by our client? I ain't trying to pry, but if I've got this wrong…"

That seemed to hit just right. Dickerhoof blinked owlishly, as though he'd forgotten the Pinkerton man waited for a response, but he puzzled through the implications of the words. Then the old man's genius took hold and a sinister smile crept free. He nodded and rose on unsteady feet. "Of course, I've got a worthy test in my workshop. It will prove… definitive. If you'd care to follow me, Mister Murdoch?"

Murdoch rose and hitched his belt. Followed the doctor to the hall, and another secure door. The dark stairs on the far side led down, into the bowels below Dickerhoof Manor. Cool, crisp air rushed through the door, a stark contrast to the sweaty stillness of the house above.

Dickerhoof led the way, one frail hand pressed against the rail. The low whine and ozone scent grew stronger, and Murdoch rested a hand upon his gun.

Men like Dickerhoof swore their genius was an innate thing, a trick of intellect or insight only they possessed. Nothing Murdoch had seen convinced him of that fact.

He'd read the books, up in Chicago. The arguments that genius was an outside force, a daemon that followed a man from birth to grave and pushed him to great lengths. An entity with goals and desires of its own, shaping the world according to its whims. In moderation, humanity harnessed the daemon and used its insights for the greater good. In those hands of those too weak, the rush of change grew dangerous.

Murdoch didn't know if that were true or not, but he'd seen

enough men like Dickerhoof repeat the same experimentsto recognise their insights weren't entirely natural.

The stairwell opened into a wide laboratory, flickering electronic lights set into the walls. Murdoch blinked. He'd grown used to such things in San Francisco, where houses hitched on the electrical systems used to keep the trolleys running, but the cost required for a private generator … well, it didn't bode well. It meant Dickerhoof's genius likely drove him past mundane concerns like money.

Or ethical qualms.

The doctor strode to a vivisection table and whipped the stained cloth free. Murdochs heart sank. He'd been prepared for patchwork figure beneath—no man who'd worked for the Pinkerton agency expected less, given the clues above—but just once it would be nice for a mad doctor to bend science towards a goal other than conquering death.

Dickerhoof gestured with the brain canister. "Behold! The triumph of science over nature!"

Murdoch beheld, but it wasn't nothing special. Another type-IV cadaver automaton waiting for a brain to get it moving.

"Don't seem like much," Murdoch said, prodding. There wasn't a mad doctor alive who didn't want to gloat when you challenged their triumphs at the right moment.

"I assure you, my dear fellow, what you see here verges upon a miracle. Halide and I hatched the theory together, of course, but my former student believed biology held the secret to conquering death. As if flesh—which had already failed us— would somehow deliver an answer nature hadn't tried already."

"So, you built a machine?"

"Nothing so simple! Wire alone couldn't connect the brain to these mechanical limbs. The true answer required a blend of several disciplines."

"You don't say," Murdoch deadpanned. "Surely, you must be a genius to unravel it all."

"Indeed!" The doctor beamed with pleasure. "We started with the writings of Galen and Avicenna, then had the vision to connect them with…"

Murdoch let the doctor ramble, noted the details he'd need to report later. Dickerhoof had taken a type four and wired it together with nerve strands instead of metal threads—original enough for the science boys in Chicago to it pull apart once the job was over.

Of course, this assumed Murdoch didn't screw up like he'd done with Nero Halide. The home office didn't like loose ends.

Dickerhoof's ramble found itself on the open trail and evolved into a full-fledged rant, touched by hysterical laughter. The faint whine plaguing Murdoch's ears grew louder and more insistent. "Observe," Dickerhoof said. "All I need to do is connect dear Lucy's head and charge the brain with sufficient current—"

Finally, Dickerhoof crossed the agency's line, and Pinkerton protocol left no doubts about what came next. Murdoch drew a pearl-handled Colt and fired; the shot echoed in the lab's tight, stone confines, the momentary deafness a blessed relief from the growing whine. He caught the Doctor in the right shoulder, and the old man fumbled the canister. He still breathed and struggled to bring up the cane, intent on triggering whatever death ray he'd concealed in the copper and quartz tip.

"Not today," Murdoch said, and fanned the trigger. Dickerhoof spun and crumpled, the Lucy's brain canister bouncing off the stone floor.

In the distance, the sharp whine built to a fever pitch. Murdock figured it for the butler, activating one or more generators, delivering the energy his master needed to return the dead to life.

The Pinkerton sighed and reloaded the colt. He collected the fallen canister and returned it to his satchel, Halide's science too dangerous to leave where anyone could find it. The butler presented a problem. Murdoch doubted the old boy understood Dickerhoof's experiments, but the Agency took no chances. Genius begat genius, after all, and Halide might not be the only student to spread Dickerhoof's strain of unconventional science. Whatever odds the butler represented, best to nip things in the bud.

Murdoch secured the satchel and raised the colt, one ear cast towards the stairwell. With luck, Nero Halide would hear Dickerhoof had taken delivery of the canister. Certainly, Murdoch had made noise in the nearby town about visiting the Manor, planting seeds to lure him in. When Halide came to claim his beloved, Murdoch could finish this godforsaken job, maybe even take a break.

But all that depended on taking the butler out, to ensure news didn't spread of Edgar Dickerhoof's passing. The generator whine vibrated Murdoch's molars as he ascended to the upper level, gun held at the ready. It might have covered the sound of a gunshot, but he wouldn't swear to it.

"Son," Murdoch bellowed from the upper door, affecting bonhomie. "I'm afraid Mister Dickerhoof's having himself a lie down. I've got a message for him, if you'd care to pass it on after I'm gone."

The butler didn't answer, and Murdoch couldn't make out footsteps over the generator's buzz. He shouldered through the upper door, braced for trouble, ready for anything Dickerhoof's hallway threw at him.

The front door hung open, exposing the front porch. Outside, the butler's tails flapped as the old boy fled across the lawn, sprinting for the stables. Murdoch fired a shot in the butler's direction, but the Colt wasn't accurate at long range, and Murdoch's hands were faster than they were steady. The butler disappeared inside the stable doors. With a weary sigh Murdoch followed, knowing the butler's lead threatened an exposure he couldn't risk. The stables burst open, and the old boy fled on a great white horse, riding bare-back and white-knuckling the mare's thick mane in his panicked attempts to get away.

"Damn," Murdoch said, and started after the fleeing servant. With luck, he could still wrap it up quick and quiet. With luck, nobody would tell tales of a Pinkerton who murdered Dickerhoof's manservant in cold blood on the road. With luck, he could still lure Halide to town, and then the manor, rather than hunt the man throughout the west a second time.

With luck, this next step could go smooth, but how long had it been since Murdoch's luck held well enough for that to be true?

"A Pinkerton never sleeps," he said, as though it might make things better.

Then he resigned himself to what still needed to be done, and scrambled for his horse.

THE DEAL

Detective Ellis Carmody parked by the graveyard abutting the Proctor Chapel, easing her cruiser onto the grassy verge beside the unsealed road. The Chapel had seen better days, the ancient stone covered with verdant moss, the graveyard gone to seed and overgrown with vines and long grass. Even the verdant greenery of the woods crew up on the building, as though it might reclaim the house of worship in a decade or two. Ellis killed the car engine and sighed, her eyes itchy and her stomach burning from too many cups of coffee. She radioed her location to Janis back at dispatch. Figured she had ten minutes before the Captain heard and got on the horn to demand answers about why she'd ignored his orders and driven all the way out here. Ellis closed her eyes and rehearsed her responses, searching for an option which might make things better.

Because Dot McAllister needs to be taken down.

Because I'm tired of you telling me to investigate what needs investigating.

Because, regardless of what we believe, McAllister thinks the Blood Stone is magic, and this was its last location.

Because my gut says this is something.

Either option had the juice. She was out here chasing ghosts and old wives' tales, while McAllister was killing her way to dominance over the local underworld. One scumbag killing another didn't bother the Captain much, especially when Ellis had five other murders on the docket.

Chill, Cap. I'm solving this one.

Ellis drew a deep breath and sighed. Stepped out into the warm night air, the hint of rain just on the horizon. She dug the warrant out of her pocket—precautionary, more than anything; by all accounts, the Proctor Chapel had been abandoned for twenty years, but all it took was one transient taking refuge to cause fourth amendment issues. She squared her shoulders and braced herself, heading for the gate in the low stone fence surrounding the Proctor Family Graveyard. She reached for the rusting metal, then halted with her fingers a few inches from the latch. An eerie silence dominated here, still and devoid of insects or birdcalls in the forest. Hackles rose on the back of Ellis Carmody's neck, and her body sensed the gunshot a split second before she heard it. She hit the dirt as the bullet whizzed past the place her head had been, streaking on to shatter the windshield of her unmarked cruiser.

Ellis swore and scrambled to the stone wall, taking cover as the second shot rang out from the treelike. A sniper, waiting for her. Protecting the Chapel. Ellis felt the *"I told you so, Cap"* swelling in her throat even as jerked her pistol clear of the holster.

The third shot ticked off the stone wall two feet shy of her position. She'd got low enough to disappear, but the sniper had her pinned down, and the thick foliage gave cover if he wanted to get a new angle. Ellis steadied her nerves and returned fire over the wall. Two shots in the rough direction of the shooter. No way either of them hit, but they'd give him something to think about, maybe delay his own attempt to move and get a better angle on her.

It bought her time, but there was no way she won a firefight from her current position. Ellis swore and debated the options: heading back to the car, or running for the church where she could hunker down until the sniper revealed himself. The fourth shot careened overhead, and Ellis decided. The car. Calling for back-up. Making an escape, if all else failed. She rolled over, shifting her weight to pull upright and make a dash. Deep breaths, gauging the ten-foot sprint she'd need to get behind the engine block. *Easy, girl. You can do this.*

She waited for the fifth shot before she rose and ran, feet churning through the soft soil of the verge. The sniper cursed— a man's voice, accented—and the sixth shot ricochetted off the road as Ellis dove over the cruiser's bonnet. She dropped low and sidled along the car, angling for the door. Gunshots rang out, punching through the chassis and shattering glass. Ellis counted them out of habit. Seven shots. Eight. A pause. Ellis figured the shooter was reloading and seized the opportunity, jerking the car door open and jerking the radio out.

"One-two-nine, one-two-nine, this is Carmody requesting back-up. I am under fire, repeat. I am—"

Two shots in rapid succession slammed into the Cruiser and Carmody flinched away. She glanced over the bonnet, searching the treelike for a target. Nothing. She brought her pistol up and waited, one eye peeking through the broken window. The sniper's new location didn't provide as much cover, and she caught a faint glimpse of red hair and a long rifle before he slipped behind a tree. Babcock, one of McAllister's thugs. Three arrests for aggravated assault, but no convictions on his record. McAllisters money bought good lawyers, and she protected her most valuable assets.

Ellis weighed her options and bluffed. "I've called for back-up," she bellowed. "Three cars are on their way here. No way you can shoot all of us."

She rested her finger against the trigger, waiting for a response. Babcock's rifle peeked around a tree trunk and she squeezed off a shot. The bullet gouged a deep wound in the bark, just shy of his location. His return fire targeted the cruiser's tires, popping front and back. The hiss of deflating inner tubes sank any hope of escaping, and she prayed the back-up she'd mentioned was arriving sooner rather than later.

"You've gotta know McAllister's going down," she shouted. "Your choice, here and now, whether you go down with her. Back-up will be here in a few minutes. If you leave now, get a head start. You can be out of the city before nightfall. Away from all the shit that's going to rain down on your boss."

The car sagged away from her as the tires exhausted their air supply. Babcock didn't fire another shot, but Ellis couldn't imagine he'd taken her off to flee the scene. Probably circling around, getting a better angle. The thick treelike gave him too many places to hide and pick her off, too much cover when he wanted to move around without being spotted.

Ellis steeled her resolve and weighed the distance to the Chapel. Sixty-three feet and the bulk of it through the overgrown, with headstones and the two-foot high fence. She'd need to duck and weave, plenty of options to pick her off, but a fast sprint would serve her better than trying to stay low amid the meager cover. Her stomach seized as the adrenaline flooded her system, and she drew a ragged breath. There were eight rounds left in her clip, and she'd empty them all on the sprint. Wild fire to discourage Babcock and buy her time to make the dust-covered windows or the chapel's heavy wooden door.

Not the smartest plan, but it beat staying put. Ellis heaved herself upright and sprinted, firing wild shots at the treelike as she ran. Babcock returned fire as she vaulted the low graveyard wall. His bullet clipped her arm, pain sparking through her as she landed hard and jinked left, dodging a gravestone. Long grass whipped her knees as she surged forward, ignoring the injury, and Babcock's bullets churned through the gravestones and soil, chasing her to the far side.

Ellis stumbled, vaulting the second fence, her balance shifting as she landed. Momentum carried her forward, and she went with it, desperately trying not to fall on her face. She brought both arms up and careened at the closest window, a stained glass depiction of the Virgin Mary with a hole in the upper right corner where a rock or bird had broken the pane. The points of her elbows shattered the glass, and she tumbled over the low sill, shards of stained glass raining on her as she hit the dusty floor and rolled. The afternoon light filtered in through the tall windows, illuminating the dust-choked pews, pulpit, and altar. Ellis hauled herself upright and thumped against the closest wall, pressing herself tight to present a smaller target.

The thick stone walls felt safe, despite the cuts and lacerations her trip through the window had opened up. The bloody wound in her right arm worried her, so she switched the gun to a two-handed grip and breathed short, ragged breaths. Babcock would need to move through the woods, maybe even break cover and cross the road to get an angle on this side of the church. It would buy her a few minutes, long enough for the back-up to arrive, assuming she didn't lose so much blood she passed out and made it easy on him.

Ellis scanned the treelike. Nothing. Her breathing slowed, letting the pain of her injuries register for the first time. She wondered if Babcock might have fled now she'd found the security of the church, realizing his window for stopping her was officially gone. She counted breaths, forcing her attention away from her wounds.

Seventy-three breaths in, Babcock surprised her by stepping clear of the trees. He carried the rifle in a low grip, ready to pull it up and fire if needed. Sweating heavily in the afternoon heat, wearing camouflage fatigues and thick military boots. Short for a hired thug. Five-nine in his heeled boots. His shock of red hair hung over his face, and his sharp eyes scanned the church. Ellis brought her gun up, but she couldn't line up the shot. Her hands shook and blood tricked down her face. A cut on her forehead, courtesy of the broken glass. She cursed beneath her breath and moved away from the window, retreating into the darkness.

Babcock paused at the edge of the graveyard. "I know you're planning on waiting this out, but nobody's coming to help you," he called. "The boss has her resources, and there's no cops but you welcome here tonight."

Ellis crawled down the space between pews, heading for the far side of the chapel.

"You're here because she wants you here," Babcock said. "This whole time, McAllister's been dropping you hints. Wanted you out here, wanted you in the church. My orders were to wing you, not take you out for good. Boss figures you're exactly who we need to get to the Stone, and we've been planning on it for a while."

Ellis hunkered behind a pew and rested both elbows against the wood, steadying her grip as she covered both the window and the church door. Babcock stepped over the low cemetery wall, advancing on the church. He didn't bring the gun up, but he looked right pleased with himself.

"I'm going to help you out, detective. The Stone's beneath the altar. Secret hiding spot. There's a latch on the bottom right. I stashed the gun I used to kill Ven Ithihara last year right in there. Everything you need to stitch me up is waiting for you, if you've got the balls to go collect it."

Ellis flicked an involuntary glance at the altar, hairs rising on the back of her neck. Babcock came to a halt in the middle of the graveyard, kneeling and bringing his rifle to bear. "Take your time, detective. I can wait all night if I've gotta."

For a moment, she contemplated trying to wait him out. Even if no backup was imminent, eventually she'd be missed by someone not on McAllister's payroll. They'd trace her phone or her car, come investigate. If she could make Babcock enter the church, the odds tipped in her favor. The rifle was good for long-range work, but her pistol made it easier to get a bead on a target in the tight confines.

Her blood dripped against the church floor, the pain growing worse. Waiting wasn't her friend.

She shoved herself onto all fours and crawled towards the altar, staying low and out of the light. Every movement kicked dust into the air, making it hard to breathe, but she found reached the pulpit and used her good arm to search. Faltering fingers found the latch and pressed down on it, her attention still focused on Babcock setting up in the graveyard.

The latch triggered a click beneath the floorboards, and a foot-long segment of the floor kicked upright. Ellis dragged herself closer and pulled it open, revealed the small cubby beneath. Babcock hadn't lied about the gun, or the cloth-wrapped jewel stashed alongside it. Ellis exhaled despite herself, fished an evidence bag out of her pocket. She lifted the gun free and set it aside, then removed the jewel with bloody fingers.

It was big. A ruby the size of a fist, perfectly cut and wrapped in waxed cloth. Her arm burned the moment she made contact, even through the durable evidence bag plastic. The pain receded like a departing tide, and her head buzzed with energy.

"You're going to want that the Blood Stone," Babcock called. "If you're smart, you'll take the deal it offers."

Detective Ellis Carmody contemplated the jewels facets. She placed it on the floor and set the evidence bag aside. Carefully, without truly knowing why, she placed a bloody finger on the stone.

The energy which flowed through her burned away any hint of pain. Shards of glass pushed free of bloody wounds, and the wounds glowed red and sealed themselves. Pressure closed on Ellis' skull, pushing in like she'd plunged to the depths of some terrible ocean. A scream surged through her throat, involuntary and shrill. The church walls shook as shadows grew long and thick, terrible claws of shadow edging up the walls and threatening to close her in a tight fist. Ellis tried to shake the jewel loose and couldn't. Her fingers refused the call to open and let the stone tumble to the floor.

The creature rose before her, a slippery mass of shadow and bone, seven feet tall and faceless. It loomed in the tight confines of the church, the featureless mass she might grudgingly think of as a head regarding her with interest. Its voice thrummed in her skull, felt rather than heard.

::I OFFER YOU A BARGAIN::

"Fuck your bargain," Ellis spat, but the words lacked the venom she'd hoped for. Dark tendrils stretched from the creature's form, caressing the sides of her skull. Brushing against the rapidly healing wounds, replacing searing pain with a desolate chill she'd never experienced.

::YOU WILL DIE HERE. YOU CRAVE JUSTICE. I WILL MAKE YOU STRONG::

Ellis attempted to speak, her tongue twisting in the voiceless echo of her mouth. The creature pulled her closer, tendrils lifting her off the dusty floor and holding her two feet off the ground.

::YOU WILL KILL THE GUILTY. YOU WILL PUNISH THE VILE::

"The guilty want me to take this deal. That's every reason to say no."

::THE ONE YOU CALL McALLISTER BELIEVES SHE MAY CONTROL YOU ONCE THE COMPACT IS DONE. SHE IS WRONG::

The scorn cracked through Ellis' skull like heavy boots stomping across thin ice.

::I OFFER YOU A BARGAIN. SERVE, OR DIE::

Ellis knew turning the creature down was the right choice. She would bleed out or get double-tapped by Babcock and the rifle. Even if she did not know what the gem had unleashed or why McAllister wanted it, making a deal with the devil to escape a tight spot was still a deal with the devil.

She'd spent her career avoiding that. Prided herself on doing things right. But a fire lit deep inside her, pushing back the cold.

A savage, eager hunger to say yes and maybe do something about the problems of the world. Take out Babcock and McAllister, save her skin and the lives of countless others, even if she damned her soul.

Ellis knew she should say no, but her heart wouldn't let her say the word.

"A compact," she said. "Agreed."

Dark tendrils plunged into her, penetrating the skin. The furious inferno of her rage waged war with the searing cold, the two sensations twisting through her like serpents fighting for domination. She gasped and fire burst from her lips, her eyes flashing red as an inferno sweated through her pores. All pain dissipated in an instant, replaced by an eager strength and rapidly healing wounds.

The tendrils withdrew, and she dropped into a crouch on the church floor.

::A COMPACT. RISE, MY CREATURE. TAKE YOUR VENGEANCE::

The celerity of her movement surprised Ellis even as she slipped from floor to window, stealing a place at Babcock's position out in the graveyard. Her heart pounded a furious tattoo, urging her out and into the fray. Ellis covered the thirty feet between them in an instant, wrenching the rifle from Babcock's grip and lifting him by the throat. The small killer's eyes flashed wide, feet kicking as he struggled to free himself from her iron grip. Ellis tossed his rifle into the woods and squeezed, strong fingers pulling tight against the soft muscle in Babcock's neck.

::KILL HIM::

Babcock let out a strangled grasp. His feet kicked twice more, then stilled. He turned blue in her grip, almost gone, and it took everything she had to pry her open and let him drop into the cemetery's long grass. Babcock huddled at her feet, coughing and gasping for air. Easy prey with her new strength and speed, filled with breakable bones and soft flesh she could rip into strips.

Ellis took a long breath and stepped back. The shadowy entity screamed in the back of her skull, demanding she follow her instincts and break the mortal at her feet.

:KILL HIM. KILL HIM. WE MADE A BARGAIN::

She produced her badge and stood over Babcock, reaching for her cuffs.

"You have the right to remain silent," she said. "Anything you say can and will be used against you in a court of law…"

Detective Ellis Carmody already ignored the orders of one captain. She figured it wasn't too hard to add a second to the list.

I'M AFRAID OF THE BIG
BAD WOLF

1.

We saw the werewolf, originally, in the summer of ninety-seven. That was the summer of getting stoned on the verandah at BJ's house. The summer I failed to finish uni. The summer the Mark of Cain released their cover of *Degenerate Boy* and it played on the radio over and over, full of heavy bass and snarling guitars and a misplaced slacker's anger that hammered along like a pneumatic drill.

Five of us in the car, on the night it all went down: me and BJ, who I haven't seen in over a decade; Hack, who's got two kids and a woman he still tells me he's going to marry one day; Speedy, who's working out of Prague these days, with rumors he's headed to Amsterdam after he finishes his latest commission. And the last guy, the one I can't remember, one of those ghosts from the past you dread appearing on Facebook, asking you to friend them without explanation.

I wrote Hack an email the other day, asking if he remembered the incident. *I've been thinking about the wolf we saw out on the way to the Seven-Eleven that night,* I said. *Jesus, we were dumb back then. Did we really need a Kit-Kat that bad? How many times did we risk our necks driving out of Tallebudgera Valley stoned?*

He didn't reply. Hack never does. None of the old gang discuss it, the night of the werewolf. None of us except me, 'cause I can't leave it alone.

2.

I no longer remember what the world looks like in daylight.

It's 2:02 AM right now. The glow of the computer screen illuminates my apartment. It's small, my place. A bed. A stove. A fridge. A desk. There are wine bottles lined up in a neat row by the computer, my private advent calendar counting down to the anniversary of when it all happened.

The Mark of Cain sounds different, coming through the computer's speakers. YouTube has eliminated the thrill of the chase.

At 3:05 AM, Natalie will finish her shift. She will leave the hospital on the far side of the city and spend a half-hour driving over here to see me. She will ask me if I've been on the internet again, bothering my former friends, trying to track down clues. I will lie, and she won't believe me, but she cannot disprove my claim.

Natalie is smart, far smarter than I am.

But me, I am wily. It's one of those traits that living with secrets instills in you.

3.

So the road out of Tallebudgera Valley is an old, winding dirt track someone covered in bitumen and said, *well, good enough, I guess*. It's easy to find your way there. From the highway you turn inland at Palm Beach, right next to the high school. Follow the road you're on and keep following it when instincts tell you to turn away. Follow it through the thin sheath of suburbs that exists between the beach and the mountains. Let the road thread you between the hills, further and further from the city. Follow it into the winding roads lined with farm paddocks and stretches of national parks. It takes less time than you'd think.

Not an easy route if you're queasy. Pplenty of tight turns and stretches where no sane person would speed.

BJ's house occupied a patch of slope way out the back of the valley, right about the point where you run out of streets. It had been his parents' place, or was his parents' place still. Either way, BJ's olds weren't around much. Or they didn't care that we were. I'm sure they were hippies once, which would explain why they didn't mind a bunch of dudes raiding their kitchen every Friday night, or people sucking down bongs on their front deck at four o'clock in the morning.

Or they minded and we ignored them, little arseholes that we were at twenty- and twenty-one. Overgrown teenagers playing at being adults, ignoring parents because that act of rebellion still felt meaningful to us.

BJ gave us the place, and I gave us the transport. I had my parent's car and a license and the lack of good sense that meant driving while blazed still seemed like an okay idea. Since BJ provided the locale every Friday, I got everyone there, doing the loop 'round the Gold Coast to pick up a disparate clan of freaks and keeping them together until it was time to drive people home on Sunday.

I wasn't cool with people getting stoned in the car, but that was my only rule. So long as I didn't pay for the fuel, I was happy to take people anywhere.

At twenty-one, in the summer of ninety-seven, I liked the idea of going places. I didn't have a job. I no longer really cared about studying. Going places held the aura of freedom, more or less.

4.

Speedy has sent me an email requesting that I cease emailing him.

He denies any memory of seeing the werewolf. *Let it go, man*, he writes. *We were seriously fucking stoned.*

I write him another email in reply, asking about his kids.

5.

Natalie shows up early, finds me seated on the edge of my bed, drinking a glass of Chardonnay. Bellarmine 2010. Not a bad drop, all things considered. She crawls into bed beside me, liberates my glass. Her head rests against my shoulder as she finds the bottle and pours.

"You're not supposed to be drinking," she says.

She drains my glass and puts it on the floor. I pretend I don't notice, keep my bare feet flat against the hardwood floor. I'm wearing underwear, black boxers and a singlet.

"You've gotta give up the wolf," Nat says.

"There's nothing to give up."

"Then you haven't spent the day on the internet, in your chat rooms."

"There are no chat rooms anymore. Chat rooms are so last decade."

"You know what I mean." She stretches, waits for me to lie beside her. Her thin arm reaches out to hold me close. "This isn't healthy. You spending all your time living in the past."

"I know."

"You gotta leave the flat some time. You need the outside world."

"I see the outside world," I tell her. "How else do I get the Chardonnay?"

"It's never a good sign when you're drinking again," she says.

"That's because you think I stop drinking." I reach across her for the glass on the floor. I drain the last of the wine. "Some days, I just hide how schnozzled I am, in the name of variety."

6.

I'm not a man who enjoys clinging to his lover, but I've learned to adapt to the heavy weight of Natalie pressed against me in the night. She smiles in her sleep, has a soft, whistling snore that marks the regular rhythm of her slumber. There are scattered freckles across her nose. There is surprising strength in her firm grip.

There is a single window in my small apartment, looking over the long downward slope of my street. Sunrise is coming and the industrious are already up and about, walking in the predawn or emerging in jogger's gear to run down the hill. Natalie will sleep for hours, so long as I am present.

I do not sleep on the nights we make love. It always brings bad dreams.

On the nights we make love, me and Natalie, I inevitably dream of the werewolf.

7.

I get the locksmith in to change all the locks in my flat. He kneels beside the doors, works at the mechanisms with an automatic drill. He lines up the screws on a flat, magnetic strip so he knows where to find them when he needs them.

He assumed that I'm crazy every time I call him out. There is a definite sense he is humoring me, the crazy hombre with a head full of wolf-dreams, simply because I have money. Five times I've called him out now, every time for the same gig. On this, his sixth trip out in an eight-month period, he shows signs that his patience is wearing thin.

We have a routine, the locksmith and me. He asks me what I'd like, and I tell him I'd like the strongest lock he has. He asks me if it's a rough neighborhood, and I tell him I have enemies.

"You mate?" he says, although the thought of me and enemies is all too much to comprehend. "Can't think of anyone hating you, eh?"

I tell him we all have enemies. They're a natural part of living.

He charges me for the new locks and shakes my hands before leaving. He is a tall man, with long hair and an inability to grow a proper goatee. It is not until his sixth visit is completed that I realize he reminds me of BJ.

8.

The night we spotted the werewolf goes like this.

We are on BJ's balcony, getting stoned, as usual. I get it into my head we need snacks. Maybe it's a thing I come up with myself. Maybe someone suggests it and keeps on suggesting until I give in. Ain't no twenty-four-hour convenience stores in walking distance, out the back of Tallebudgera Valley. The nearest seven-eleven is a forty-minute drive away—back through the Valley's winding roads and straight on 'til you hit the beach—and we're all pretty baked by the time the idea sets in. So the idea of snacks bounces around my head—Seven-Eleven hotdogs and a bottle of Jolt cola, food of the gods when you're twenty and dumb—and getting there doesn't seem like too big a deal. I mean, sure, I'm a *little stoned*, but I'd driven stoned before, right?

The others, they know the score when I do this shit. They're pondering food too, and how much cash they've got in their wallets, whether they've got enough to pay for fuel to the store and back. They do a whip around, figure they've got enough; pack themselves into my parent's car while the guys without cash hang out and keep playing Sonic.

And I put the keys in the ignition, turn up the stereo, and drive. *Degenerate Boy* is playing. All of us are singing along. I don't put my younger years on a pedestal. I don't long for the days when music was better, or pine for the friendships of youth. If you ask me, high-school was a torture I endured for five years, and those early years of Uni were more of the same. I lingered on the Gold Coast for far longer than anyone should, and self-loathing was the price I paid for staying there.

But that drive out of Tallebudgera Valley, stoned, using the radio and screamed conversation to keep ourselves awake, that was something worth living for. A drowning man clings to the life raft he finds, no matter how slight, you know?

So we drive. I turn up the stereo 'cause it means I don't have to listen to the other guys spinning shit. We're barely on the road before we're all screaming the lyrics 'cause there's nowhere else you can scream. Even now, there are so few places to scream in life.

We all need to scream sometimes.

The wolf finds us halfway out of the valley, right in the middle of a straight stretch. A bit of road bordered by barbed wire fences on both sides, separating us from the paddocks full of cows. We're halfway out, just starting up the hill, when it appears in the headlights.

A big, fuck-off-motherfucker sized wolf sitting on the edge of the road.

I know how it sounds. It was late. It was dark. I was stoned and my adrenaline was running and when I say things like *it was a wolf as big as the car, man,* there's all sorts of reasons to believe that my mind was playing tricks on me. I've had the arguments with myself, telling myself it was just a dog that grew larger and weirder through a trick of the light. That Australia doesn't have ordinary wolves, let along the supernatural kind that roam around when the moon is full.

Five of us in that car, and when we spotted the wolf, there wasn't any doubt. It was a fucking wolf, and it made us loose our collective minds. A simultaneous outbreak of collective hysteria. Only once in my life have I ever truly floored the accelerator in my car, slamming my foot down and generating all the speed I could get out of the small engine.

It happened that night. I don't even remember doing it, or how we avoided dying when we hit the curves in the road. All I remember is getting away, coming down off the adrenaline, the nervous laughter that filled the car when I turned the radio down and checked if everyone was okay.

One guy—memory says it was Speedy, but memory is unreliable—asked the question: "What the fuck was that?"

And BJ said, real simple: "I think it was a werewolf, man."

And if we hadn't been thinking about it before those words, we all thought about it after. It made a kind of terrible sense: Australia doesn't have wolves, so there wasn't much reason to see one roaming wild. It might have been a dog, I guess, but a dog doesn't make a bunch of people lose their minds.

Our minds hadn't coped with the encounter. It was trying to fill the gaps with stuff that made sense of all the data. Terms like werewolf gave us something to latch onto, even as we tried to react the idea.

9.

Through it all, I kept driving. We made it to the Seven-Eleven, stocked up on supplies, and spent a half-hour driving aimlessly instead of heading back. None of us said words like *scared*, but fuck it, that's what we were. We were rational kids; geeks of one sort or another. We'd seen something we couldn't explain, and it left its mark on us, a mark that lingered until the jokes started: silver; wolfsbane; staying down by the beach until the full moon was done with. Give fear a name and you can get past it, coat it in a veneer of civilization that eventually becomes more than that.

And so we drove back to BJ's place and delivered the snacks to the other guys. We didn't see the werewolf on the way back and we didn't talk about it afterward. After that half-hour, driving aimlessly, none of us ever used the word *werewolf* again, not even to each other.

Except me.

10.

I wake after dark and go to Youtube. I make coffee, which I do not drink, and open a bottle of wine, which I do.

Natalie is in Canberra. Attending a conference. Talking to a specialist. I chat with a guy online who lives down Canberra way. He claims to have photographs of werewolves in the wild, documented proof of their existence. He's willing to sell them for one hundred dollars a photograph on the condition that they are acquired in person.

I tried to convince Natalie to act as my go-between. His response makes me wonder if I'll see her on her return. I want to call her, but I do not dial her number. I finish my wine. I let my coffee cool. I listen to my songs on YouTube, over and over again.

I know how it will go from here, now I've pushed Natalie too hard and asked her to do something she hates. The next few weeks will be unpleasant, a slow deterioration of the status quo that allows us to stay together. Natalie will press me to get help, to talk to someone about what happened. I will refuse, and there will be fights. She will spend the night at her place. I will drink more Chardonnay. She will call less, and I don't call at all, and soon we will break up.

The photographs will be rubbish, unconvincing detritus assembled by a disturbed mind. No proof werewolf exists at all, or a hastily photoshopped image. This isn't my first rodeo, but I keep pushing. I need to understand how it all slipped away because of something so small, a werewolf that didn't even attack.

I need to know why I can't walk away, even though I want to. Even though things would be so much better if I left it all int he past.

11.

On the anniversary, I hire a car and drive down to the Gold Coast. I follow the highway down the shoreline, turn right at Palm Beach. This sounds easy, but it's not. It involves a train ride to the airport, where I hire a car. It means remembering how to talk like a human being as I approach the counter and give them my license. The music on the stereo is unfamiliar, a melange of beats and whining that mixes into an auditory slur.

I drive through the winding roads, past the farms and stretches of national park. I find the low curve a few minutes away from BJ's place. It's a shallower bend than I remember. There are farmhouses visible in the distance. Their lights are on. There are Utes out the front.

There are horses in the paddock closest to my car. They walk over, poke their noses over the barbed wire, taking an interest in my presence. Their heavy breathing overtakes the quiet tick of the engine. One of them lowers its head to chew on the grass by my feet.

I pull out my phone and start taking pictures. The ancient Nokia beeps and clicks. Legacy sound effects, to make old bastards like me feel better about the future. The flash seems to startle the horses, but they do not bolt. They just glare at me, like I've done something wrong.

I sit on the bonnet and flick through my photographs. They don't really help any. They show nothing. Empty fields. A white commodore. Three horses with a farmhouse visible in the background. Half a shot of the curving road, obscured by a close-up of my thumb.

Speedy went to university. Packed up and moved to Melbourne in order to do an arts degree, disappearing into a world that seemed unfamiliar to the rest of us. He showed up on the coast from time to time, visiting his parents and catching us on the way through. University changed him, though. He'd become a different kind of geek, focused on making big art that none of us really understood. I see his work out there, sometimes, when I brave the world.

BJ disappeared, the way old friends tend to. Last I heard, he'd become a hermit in the house his parents owned, just 'round the corner from that same curve in the road. But that was a long time ago, and my source is hardly reliable. BJ's the only one of us who never appeared on Facebook, which is a victory of a kind, I guess.

Hack stayed Hack. He went to Sydney, after we saw the werewolf, got married and started having kids. Hasn't bothered to come home, doesn't accept Friend requests from any of us on the various social medias. I got his email via a mutual acquaintance, but he never responds.

The other folks I knew in that era, I couldn't really tell you about. I didn't care then, and I don't care now. They were just guys, you know? People in the background. Acquaintances, rather than friends.

It would have been easier if it had attacked us. If the werewolf had leapt upon the car and tore holes through the roof. Ripped BJ or Hack apart, left them bloodied on the side of the road while the rest of us escaped. Violence leaves an obvious mark, but it wasn't violence that got us.

As the sun sets and the moon rises, I tromp over to the stretch of grass where the werewolf crouched by the side of the road. I stand there, right on the spot it happened, on the place where the world as I knew it died for reasons I couldn't place. I stand there for two straight hours, thinking about the guys I used to know. The friends lost, the lifetime whittled away looking for more detail.

As predicted, Natalie is gone. All I've got left is the chase. To my surprise, hot tears stain my cheeks, and I cannot make them stop. I cock an ear, listening for the howl of wolves, trying to hold back a scream.

As the full moon rises low and heavy over the horizon, I finally give voice to the turmoil burning inside me.

It comes out as a lonely, mournful howl and it doesn't satisfy me.

OR FOR ETERNITY HOLD YOUR PIECE

Jack took point on the mezzanine, huddled against a stone pew, praying none of the assembled monsters recognized a mortal in their midst.

The nuptials of Vorta of the Phospherine Sisters and Tal Lukesha of the Blood were the supernatural event of the season. Jack's recognised dozens of entities on his crew's hit list among the guests. Hell, down on the lower level, there were pews set aside for the spectral attendees, which opened the chance there'd be a few they'd actually succeeded in killing showing up to pay their respects.

Jill's voice buzzed in his ear, carried over the sub-dermal mics. "This is what you'd call a target rich environment, yes?"

"Eyes on the prize," Jack whispered. "There's only two entities with apocalyptic potential today, and it all takes to trigger the end of the world is the words 'I do'."

"Piece of cake," Jill said. "We've fought tougher crowds than this."

Pure bravado to cover the nerves. Jack felt it too, but you couldn't get by on bravado. "Just found us a way out. This crowd's going to riot the moment we open fire."

The mic went dead and Jack caught a glimpse of Jill up in the orchestra pit. Dressed to blend in with the band, her sniper rifle in the trombone case. Enough ammo to soften Tal Lukesha up and get Jack close enough to kill the prick before things progressed too far.

In a lot of ways, Jill had the tricky job. Slipping away from the band and getting into the rafters, finding an angle from where she could line up her shot and call the play without getting noticed. There were bat folk in the fourth row, scanning the room with sonar. Countless entities with telepathy or a sense of smell so keen they'd pick up the gun oil on the rifle or the adrenaline surging through Jill's system.

But the rafter's meant Jill could get out clean, even if they discovered her. It gave her distance from the fray, and Jack could summon the Summer Sword at will, call it to his hand when it was time to kick ass and wade his way towards the altar. They'd studied the plans for the Blood Cathedral, laid out a dozen plans and failsafes, but none of it changed the simple equation: killing Lukesha put Jack in a chamber packed to the gills with stronger, faster, and more dangerous entities, and there was no way out before the guests ripped him to shreds once the job was done.

Jack had protested they'd find a way once they were on the ground. That's how he'd talked Jill and the others to go along with the mission. Truthfully, this was a suicide run. His promise to hold back if they couldn't find an opening was an empty thing, a fiction so Jill could live with doing her part.

He'd lost track of her while absorbed in his thoughts, but Jill's voice buzzed in his ear once more. "I'm in position. There's a mind reader on the bride's side of the aisle, so don't go looking for me."

"Roger that. You see anything we might have missed during the prep?"

"Stained glass window by the altar, half-hidden behind the curtain."

It was a lead-stained thing the size of a cellar door. The art depicted the Blood Clan's sinking of Atlantis, the ancient city disappearing beneath crashing waves. Jack knew it might be there, regardless of their prep. It didn't appear on maps, but a sketch of it appeared in the Chronicles of Darus . The Chronicles included a rumor the window led straight to the Strangling Abyss, where the great old one's slumbered and awaited the end of all things.

That made it a risky choice. "Playing alarm clock for ancient gods isn't an improvement on what we're trying to stop," Jack said.

"Then you're out of luck, and we call this off," Jill said. "No point getting killed here, Jackie."

Down on the altar, a wizened blood priest emerged from the vestry.

"Game face on," Jack said. "It's showtime."

The decrepit priest hobbled to the altar and Tal Lukesha rose, eight imperious feet tall, long horns casting a fearsome shadow. The demonic warlord dwarfed the priest, but the hollow eyes and lips sewn shut with crimson thread leant the celebrant a more terrifying air. He spread his palms wide, espousing the tooth maw set into each hand, and signaled for all to rise. A low, discordant tune accompanied the bride's entrance, Vorta of the Phospherine Sisters escorted down the aisle by twelve of her sisterhood, all armed and armored for battle. The bride's long veil and ragged ground scraped along the cobbled floor, and the priest welcomed her.

The twin mouths set into his hand spoke in unison. "Dreadful beloved, we have gathered here today to witness the bloody union of…"

Years of practice let Jack tune the sermon out. With psychics and mind-readers in the crowd, it was best to go on autopilot and let instinct and training take over. Check out of all conscious thought and do what needed doing.

Twenty years he'd been doing this. He had the job down by now. Pity this was the last job, but it was a hell of a way to go.

The Blood Priest ran bride and groom through the ceremony, every eye on the pustule-faced demon warrior and the severe, red-haired witch who spelled doom for the world.

Jack lets the words wash over him, calm and ready to move once the Blood Priest asked: "If any entity in this room knows a good reason these two should not form a union, speak now or for eternity."

Jack prepared to rise, forming the image of the Summer Sword in his mind's eye. Instinct would carry him over the mezzanine and down to the ground floor, towards the altar and the waiting demon.

Then: "I object."

Jack startled, his concentration lost. One of the War-Wolves of Amalekites stood, making their case. "I object," he howled, "for they betrothed the witch to me."

Steel cleared scabbard as the wolf-man drew his blade, and all eyes swung towards him. "I am the wolf destined to devour the moon and end the world, and I will fight for my bride."

The blood priest gaped, toothy maw gasping soundless words. Vorta of the Phospherine Sisters demurred, her response inscrutable behind the tattered veil.

Her husband to be wasted no time in making himself clear. "The Dread Wolf lies," Tal Lukesha bellowed. "The bride is mine by right of conquest."

"They promised her to me!" Another cry, from the back. Jack craned his head along with the rest of the crowd, spotted the Ghadir Crowlord perched in the back row. A lesser warlock, barely powerful enough to stand against Tal Lukesha alone, and likely choosing this moment to stake his claim because the demon already had a challenger.

"You?" Tal Lukesha snorted.

The Crowlord stood his ground. "I had business with the sisterhood, and she was the price for my services. They will not deny me what's mine by right."

Jill's voice echoed in Jack's ear. "This your doing, boss?"

"Nope, but we can use it. Wait for my signal."

"Rodger Rodger."

Down on the floor, the War Wolf advanced on the stage, the Crowlord tailing after him. Tal Lukesha shrugged off his formal jacket, exposing the scar covered torso, legacy of a thousand battles. Long claws jutted forth from his bare hands, and he met the oncoming suiters with a grim smile.

The War Wolf struck first, lashing out with the cold iron blade that whistled through the air. Tal Lukesha ducked sideways, out of range, then darted in to strike. The wolf howled in pain, reversing his swing and pressing the advantage against the demon. Across the Blood Church, visitors got to their feet, angling for a better look. Some departed, preferring not to be too close to the conflict.

Jack flashed a quick grin, activated his throat mic. "Chaos will make it harder for mind-readers to pick up on our plans. Let me get to the ground floor, then sew a little chaos."

Jill didn't respond, but he trusted her to do her part. Jack slipped free of the pews and ghosted his way to the stairs leading down, fighting against the flow of bodies to get to the bottom floor. The Priest cast his eyeless gaze about, trying to follow the clash of steel and claw, and Jack spotted the Crowlord up on the altar, trying to fight his way past the Phospherine sisters to get to Vorta.

A silence gunshot streaked through the air and splattered one of the honor-guard's brains over the stained altar. A second shot winged the bride herself, drawing out a wild shriek of pain and fury that reminded Jack of shattering glass.

He focused his thoughts and imagined the Summer Sword, the comfortable weight of the blade in his hand. Jill fired a third time and took down another Sister. The Crowlord fell back, scrambling on his heels until he found cover behind the altar. In the main aisle, the War Wolf and Tal Lukesha wheeled, trying to find an angle that would allow them to gut the other.

They'd need to take out all three suitors if they wanted to keep the world safe. Jack leapt into the fray, his sword materializing out of thin air as he whipped one hand around. The blade appeared, bright as the midday sun and hotter than baked pavement, cutting through the War Wolf's hide with ease. Black, fetid blood spurted from the wound and Tal

Lukesha wasted no time in claiming the advantage, dispatching the wolf with claws thrust into the neck.

"One down," Jack said, but Tal Lukesha wasted no time before swatting at the Summer Sword. Bullets rained down from the rafters, throwing the demon off-balance, and Jack seized the advantage. He plunged the Summer Sword into the broad chest, the burning point sizzling through the pustules and piercing a black heart. Tal Lukesha grunted, blood spilling from his maw, and the demon pitched forward like a falling tree.

On the far side of the altar, the Crowlord fought with the honor guard of Phospherine Sister. The blood priest cast its eyeless gaze in Jack's direction, standing side-by-side with the bride.

"INTERLOPER!" The rasp of the Blood Priest's howl cut through the chaos of the room, and Jack spun to face the assembled guests, Summer Sword held in a two-handed grip.

"Sixty-three entities between you and the door," Jill supplied. "I'm bugging out."

"Meet you at the safe-house," Jack whispered.

Pure bravado, to cover the nerves. He swung the Summer Sword in a lazy arc, its golden light filling the blood church with a warmth that verged on sacrilege. The Blood Priest covered its empty sockets and hissed through both palms.

Myriad eyes fixed upon him, everyone waiting for someone else to make the first move and start the assault. Jack flashed them all a cocky smile. "For the record, I object too. No way this marriage should go ahead."

It was Vorta of the Phospherine Sisters who broke the impasse, pointing a finger at Jack and unleashing a banshee hour that rattled his molars. The Crowlord responded, striding across the altar as though dispatching the assassin would earn him the bride. Jack lunched, blade slicing across warlock's stomach, and it took the fight out of him in an instant.

For a moment, the Blood Church went still, silent except for the Crowlord's coughing and attempts to hold his insides in place. Then the remaining sixty-two entities howled as a collective, surging like a single living organism intent on ripping

Jack apart. He ducked and weaved between them, focused only on the exit, the Summer Sword flashing left and right, lopping off hands and slicing away flesh. As entities fell, he kept a count: one dead, two dead, three dead, four.

Only fifty-eight entities to go before he could get away, but at least the world was safe for another day.

SIX CATS GO CAMPING

The fire already burned in the tangled clearing. A cool breeze wound through the forest and tugged at the flames, trying to lure it closer to the fallen log that bifurcated the open space. Foolish, but the wind is foolish sometimes. Willing to burn an entire forest just to warm her frozen hands.

Moonbelly slunk from the darkness with a caution that belied her size. Big for a cat, and well-fed. Black as soot and emerald eyed, with a crescent of pale fur that curved against her stomach. She crossed the clearing, sniffing the broad rocks and thatches of grass, skirting the fire until she'd satisfied herself no danger waited to leap out. Once done, she flopped by the ring of stones, stretching her paws towards the flames.

The campfire always burned here, on the nights they all attended, and the scent of wood smoke lingered weeks after the meetings. A cold and lonely kind of magic, or so Starwalker claimed.

Moonbelly had neither the knowledge or the desire to contradict her friend.

The others arrived slowly, in dribs and drabs. Foglick first, the gray-furred stray slinking through the gap between oaks on the north side. He loped onto the ancient log and walked its length, leapt to a large rock on the far side of the clearing and settled there, draping one paw over the edge. He stared at

Moonbelly's exposed stomach, ears high and whiskers taut. In another place, another time, the stray might have pounced and attempted a fight, even if he were naught but fur and bones compared to Moonbelly's well-fed frame.

The kittens came next, scampering through the forest as a pair, playing tag among the roots and leaves. Skitterclaw— ginger-furred, wide-eyed, with stockinged feet—and his butter-furred sister Daffodil. They darted into the clearing, Daffodil chasing Skitterclaw into the warmth, and both halted as though surprised to find the fire burning and others waiting.

Skitterclaw pulled his ears back and eyed Foglick's perch with apprehension. "Are we late?"

Foglick met the question with a snort, and Moonbelly rolled over and fixed a lazy eye on the stray, just in case he forgot himself. Daffodil sidled up beside her brother, butted her head against his shoulder. "We can't be late," she said. "I don't see Starwalker, or Elmshadow. We can't be late if we're not the last ones here."

Skitterclaw's whiskers rippled with worry. "Perhaps they're hiding. A smart cat hides while waiting."

"Or they might not come." Foglick's long tail lashed against his stone perch, a rapid tattoo of irritation. "Perhaps it's all for naught tonight."

Skitterclaw crouched low, ears flat. He eyed Foglick and edged backwards, retreating from the stray's withering stare. Foglick survived on the streets and the wild, and Skitterclaw had spent his first year in the warmth and comfort of a home with regular fires and wet, gushy food and warm humans to lie against when the nights were cold. His eyes darted from Foglick to Moonbelly, searching for assurance. "They wouldn't not come," he said. "He wouldn't do that to us."

"It may not be their choice," Foglick said. He stretched a paw towards the flame and yawned, affecting nonchalance at the thought that so distressed the smaller cat. "They might have been eaten by bears, or trapped in the dens of their tall folk. They might have crossed a witch and been cursed to forget us all."

Skitterclaw squeaked, his ears working back and forth in a panic, and Foglick fixed the smaller cat with a look of pure disdain. Moonbelly rolled to her feet, careful not to stare too hard and offer Foglick a challenge. "They'll come," she said. "They hear the call, same us the youngling. And same as you, Foglick. Even if they'd been cursed, they'd come for that."

"Yeah!" Daffodil sidled up to her brother's shoulder. Defiance ran through the small kitten, her blue eyes resolute as she met Foglick's glare. A foolish, foolish choice if you asked Moonbelly, and she tensed in case Foglick took issue with the youngling's bravado. The threat of violence shimmered in the air, and Daffodil hunkered down, ready to launch herself into a fight with the larger, stronger stray.

Moonbelly knew who would win that fight, even if Skitterclaw steeled himself to aid his sister. She considered her methods of intervention, and ultimately rolled onto her back to wave all four paws in the air, swatting at the stars and the embers coughed up by the fire. Playing the fool was not to every cat's taste, but it diverted attention from the fight. All eyes turned on her, trying to gauge why she'd chosen to expose her soft underbelly, wondering if she was mad.

"They'll come," Moonbelly repeated. She stretched a leg, paw splayed wide, and admired the bright stars above.

Foglick knew what she'd done and snorted his disgust. "Perhaps they won't this time. They've never been this late before."

"He's right," Skitterclaw said. "They're late. They might not come at all."

Moonbelly paused in her play, all too aware of what that meant. Foglick pushed himself upright, unblinking eyes never leaving Skitterclaw's frightened face. His whiskers rippled with irritation, but he settled onto the rock once more, and turned toward the flames. Done with the too-and-fro of questions, and content to let things go.

Best to distract the kittens before they fouled things up again. Moonbelly writhed against the grass. "Itch," she said. "At the base of my tail."

Skitterclaw prowled to a small copse of long grass and hunkered low, still as the night sky. Foglick groomed his paw, chewing at the soft pad, while Daffodil's attention drifted to the moths fluttering towards the fire.

"I'm bored," she declared, and leapt at a passing moth. It zigzagged free and her feet whispered against the grass, curling and pouncing again. This time she caught the moth and hunched over it. She looked up, meeting their eyes in turn, justifiably proud of her kill. "I'm really bored. Can't we start?"

A voice from the darkness said, "No, we wait."

They all turned as Starwalker emerged from the darkness. A piebald cat with mismatched eyes, he moved with slow and cautious grace. "It's proper to wait, and we need six."

"But I've got a great story," Daffodil whined. She chewed on the moth and swallowed, then looked around, staring at her fellow felines. "A true story, about my mother, and the time she went out onto the black-stone path and battled a snarling beast—"

"Why would mother go out on the black-stone path?" Skitterclaw asked.

His pale eyes were wide with fear, and Daffodil whirled with excitement at the prospect of answering him. "Because she wanted—"

"No." Starwalker drew himself up, proud and proper. He lacked the heft of Moonbelly or the lean muscle of Foglick, but he carried himself like a hunter, undaunted by the size or speed of his prey. It's said he served a witch, once, before he found his current home. "We wait," he said. "It's proper that we wait."

Daffodil sighed and flopped onto the grass. "But I'm bored."

"We're all aware," Foglick said. "You've declared it twice now, and our hearing is good."

"Doesn't make it any less true," Daffodil said. Another moth flew by and she batted a lazy paw in its direction, but the game had lost its appeal now.

"I'm going to tell a story about the river," Skitterclaw said. "I can watch it from the window on a bad day, gray as Foglick's fur and dark as the last soul."

"Are there fish?" Moonbelly said.

"I don't know."

Moonbelly twisted and cocked her head. "Why not?"

"I've never been close," Skitterclaw said. "It scares me, and it goes on forever."

"Nothing goes on forever." Foglick rumbled his voice like he was preparing to roar.

"The river does," Skitterclaw said. "It does in my story."

"It needs a toad." Moonbelly said. She puffed her chest, whiskers shivering. "I caught a toad once, next to the pond in my garden. It offered me that magic stone in its head if I promised to let it go."

Skitterclaw's eyes grew wide. "What did you do with it?"

"I killed it and took it to my tall folk," Moonbelly said. "What use do I have for a magic stone?"

Starwalker jumped onto a log and let a single paw dangle down, the white fur on his toes oddly pink in the firelight. "I have a simple story," he said, yawning. "One that started long ago, one that ends badly, but it is a story none-the-less."

"Does it have mice?" Moonbelly asked, and once again Foglick snorted. Moonbelly fixed him with an icy stare. "I enjoy hearing about mice."

"That's because you're always hungry," Foglick said. "And you've lost too much to the tall folk who feed you."

Moonbelly shrugged the insult off. There was naught to prove to Foglick, and she cared not for his pride. "Mice are good eating," she said, and turned her gaze to Starwalker. "So, are there mice?"

"There are no mice. Just a house, and a few cats, and the tall folk that belonged to them."

"Houses usually have mice," Moonbelly's stomach lets out a low rumble, part purr and part hunger.

"They do," Starwalker said. "This one doesn't. Not in my story."

"Doesn't sound like much of a story," Foglick rumbled. "And Elmshadow is still late. No-one may end up telling stories tonight."

"Perhaps you should mind your tongue," a deep voice rumbled from the darkness. Five heads swung to the shadows, whiskers alert, watching the giant cat emerge. His fur was all tortoise-shell and scars, his left eye milky and blind.

"About time," Foglick said. Skitterclaw nodded in agreement.

"I'm right on time," Elmshadow said. "It's the rest of you who are early."

Foglick exposed his teeth, but thought better of making a scene. Tough as the stray was, he'd fought fewer battles than Elmshadow, and even speed and youthful strength would not carry him against the wealth of experience Elmshadow possessed.

The scarred cat strolled into the clearing and rubbed his head against Moonbelly, then touch noses with both the younglings. Foglick watched Elmshadow, and Starwalker watched Foglick, and everybody knew they wouldn't fight now, not once they'd gathered and it was time to start.

Skitterclaw cleared his throat. "Shall we begin?"

"I'll go," Foglick said. The other cats raised their ears in alarm.

"It's Elmshadow's night," Starwalker said. "He either claims the right to tell a story, or picks who tells one if he's got naught to share."

"Unless you want to fight him for it," Daffodil said.

Foglick looked from cat to cat, eyes slit and tail sweeping. His fur rippled as muscles set, ready to leap, then rippled again as he settled into a crouch. "Then perhaps Elmshadow should start," he said. His pink tongue darted out, testing the air. "The night won't last forever and I can already I can taste dawn coming."

Elmshadow settled back on his haunches, twisting his whiskers in quiet amusement.

"If it's my turn, and my choice, I'd rather tell a story," he said. "If you're all ready, I'll begin."

. . .

Once upon a time, *Elmshadow said,* when your mother's mother was still living her first life, a female of the tall folk moved into a house full of ghosts. It was the kind of house you would describe as ramshackle, full of creaking walls and drafty floors, but the female had inherited it from her grandmother and loved it beyond all else. She told herself that the house had character, a carefully wrong lie that allowed her to ignore the dusty corners and the long hall full of memories. Mostly, she stayed because it was her place, this house of ghosts and sadness. She was drawn to it as cats are drawn to the moon.

Every day, the female would walk through the house, exploring the quiet rooms that were lit by sunlight pushing its way through the dirty windows. Every night she would lie in her small bed, the same bed she used to sleep in when she visited her grandmother's house as a girl, and she would dream wild dreams of darkness and despair. And through it all, the ghosts would cluster around her, pale as a funeral shroud. They clung to her like fleas, gaunt fingers wrapping in her hair, white lips tasting her joy and her sorrow with careful kisses and silent nibbles.

They tasted of her, the ghosts of the house, and they siphoned from her everything they needed to survive. The sad ghosts would steal her joy, savoring her reactions to a dew-stung spider web or the flowering recollection of her grandmother's kindness. The angry ghosts stole her peace, carefully eroding the quiet place of calm that existed deep in her soul. The lonely ghosts stole her love, first the dwindling embers of her feelings for fresh-faced men, then the soothing coals of daughterly affection she felt when she thought of her grandmother's cool hands. They tasted of her, the ghosts of the house, stole from her with greedy abandon, until they left the female with nothing but sorrow and rage and hate. She carried all the feelings the ghosts had no use for, plus a few dying embers of love for the house that they never actually stole, a token longing that ensured she would never leave.

So the female stayed in the house of her grandmother, growing sadder and sadder as the days passed by. Some days, without warning, she would cry, weeping quietly over the purple chair in the library or sniffling as she dug through the box of paper-skinned onions in the pantry. Still the ghosts clung to her, greedily sucking and nibbling, as though they could get to the very marrow of her soul.

Friends and family would visit her, offering her advice.

"You should move," they told her. "Living here isn't healthy. Look how pale you've gotten."

But she ignored them, and she stayed, and the ghosts took more from her with every passing day. Her friends stopped visiting first, frustrated by the wall of sadness they couldn't penetrate. Eventually her family left her to her grief, unable to stomach the gnawing loneliness that ate at them when they visited and drank tea in the sad little parlor on the north side of the house.

The female was left along alone, lost, angry at a world that had taken her grandmother away from her. She stopped wandering the house, stopped getting lost in the memories that made her melancholy. She simply stayed in her room, listening to records on her grandmother's aging gramophone. And so things went for a year, with the sorrow and the ghosts and the lonely music.

And so things would have stayed, had the cat not arrived on her doorstep.

It was not a handsome cat, as we would measure such things. It arrived on a stormy night, driven onto the porch of the house by the welter of the rain. Its dark fur was sodden and tangled, its whiskers soaked with drops of water, its voice reduced to a hoarse yowl by the wet and the cold. It was a small cat, obviously the runt of its litter, and it climbed the stairs with a limp, unsure of its footing.

It was the ghosts that noticed it first, sitting on the doorstep. A sodden cat, little more than a kitten, desperately licking itself in a futile effort to arrange its inky fur. They turned their attention from the female in order to consider it.

"Oho," murmured the largest of the ghosts. "A visitor; too weak to flee. We shall dine well tonight."

A chorus of agreement rippled through the assemblage.

"It's sick," muttered a ghost with vacant eyes. "Listen to it wheezes and sneeze. It will be one of us before too long."

Several ghosts coughed their agreement, phlegm-choked voices thick with the illnesses that claimed their life.

"It's a cat," rasped a bespectacled ghost, the wisest of the brood. "Cats are always trouble."

None of them paid the bespectacled ghost any heed, his voice drowned out by coughs and murmurs and chortles of glee. They swarmed over the doorstep, gathering around the small cat as it scratched three times at the emerald door of the house.

"Let me in," the cat said. "It's cold."

Its green eyes looked up at the ghosts, peering into the miasma of pale forms that cloaked the stairwell.

"You can see us?" said the largest of the ghosts. "That's impossible. No living creature can see the dead."

"I'm a cat," the cat said. "We do not recognize the impossible. Let me in."

The cluster of ghosts laughed and howled at the cat's bravado, their pale fingers dancing as they mocked the sodden creature.

"Only someone who's living can open this door," whispered the ghost with vacant eyes, "and she who lives here will never hear you unless we will it."

"I am a cat," said the cat. "Nothing is forbidden to me. Let me in."

The ghosts drew closer, looming over the ragged kitten with hunger and longing in their eyes.

"We should eat him fast," the bespectacled ghost rasped. "Eat him now, before he causes trouble."

The other ghosts howled their agreement, diving forward with arms outstretched. Their voices rose in a dreadful cacophony, howling like the shrill wind of the storm.

"I am a cat," the cat whispered. "You will not dine on me."

Then the cat let loose a great yowl, loud enough to rattle the cracked windows and shake the dusty floors. A great yowl so loud that the ghosts scattered in fear, fleeing back into their darkened hidey-holes and their lurking shadows. A great yowl so loud that even the female of the tall folk, sitting lonely and forlorn in her bed, heard the creature and opened the emerald door to find out what was causing the ruckus.

The cat lay on the doorstep, thin chest barely rising as it gasped for breath, its energy spent by the call.

"Look at you," the female said. "You're soaked through."

The cat made a small noise in the back of its throat, a tiny mew of agreement. It looked up at the female, opening its green eyes wide in a silent plea.

"You'd best come in," the female said, picking up the sodden cat and stroking its tangled fur. The cat curled in her arms, rubbing its head against her chest, letting its purr sink into the lonely places of the female's heart and give her something more than sorrow to contemplate. The female carried the cat inside and placed it beside the fireplace. She rubbed it down with one of her grandmother's tattered towels, recovered from a long unopened closet. She stroked its drying fur, scratching the thin belly with idle fingers. She sat quietly and watched as the cat curled up in front of the fire, its rumbling purr merging with the steady crackle of the flames.

"I guess you can stay the night," the female said. "But it's probably best if you leave in the morning. This isn't a suitable house for a kitten."

The cat sneezed at her, once, twice, thrice, before laying its tail over its nose and closing its bright green eyes.

"Good night," the female said, but the cat was already asleep.

The cat slept for hours by the fireplace, warming itself in the dull heat of the coals. It woke when the clock tolled out its midnight charm, twelve resonant tones that filled the halls of the house and rumbled out from there. Though the cat did not open its eyes, it could sense the presence of something in the room with the faintest flick of a whisker. A dozen somethings, perhaps a hundred somethings, all waiting for the cat to awake.

The young cat smiled a secret smile. It opened one eye and looked around.

It was surrounded by ghosts, dozens of pale bodies floating through the dusty air. They were luminous in shadows of midnight, their shapes held together with whispers and memories.

"I was sleeping," the cat said. "You had no right to wake me."

"This is our house," said the tallest of the ghosts. "We do as we please."

The cat looked at the tallest of the ghosts, considering him with pale green eyes.

"I like it here," the cat said. "This is my house now, and you have no place in it."

A chortle of glee ran through the mass of ghosts, a ghastly sound that reminded the cat of a panicking toad.

"You cannot claim this place, little puss," said the ghost with vacant eyes. "It's ours, and we give it away to nobody."

"I could take it," the cat said. "You know that such a thing is possible, should a cat be determined to claim something as their own."

"We could stop you," the ghosts chorused. "We would stop you. This place is ours." Then they made frightening faces, gouging out their eyes and flaying their own flesh, trying to frighten her. The young cat simply yawned.

"You're dead," the cat said. "It is poor form for the dead to trouble a cat. Go away, it's time I was asleep once more."

"If we're dead," said the ghost with glasses, "what do we have to lose?"

"Everything has something to lose," the cat said. "Even a ghost."

Then the cat stretched, working its back and legs in turn, before spinning three times around its place by the fire and settling down. The ghosts lingered, making ghoulish faces and taunting with gurgling voices, but the young cat simply ignored them and went back to sleep.

That night, the ancient house was a place of dreams. The female dreamt of a scrawny kitten that frolicked with her through the bright halls and warm rooms of her childhood, dreamt of the grandmother that filled the room with the smell of cookie dough and talcum powder, dreamt of a nearly forgotten childhood memory when she found a leprechaun's treasure of chocolate coins hidden at the bottom of a rainbow in a cow paddock. The female woke up humming, the taste of a dozen chocolate coins on her tongue and the smell of talcum powder in the air. Then, for the first time that she could remember, the female smiled. When she went downstairs, the cat was waiting. The female offered the cat a meal of warm milk and sardines, both of which the young cat ate, because a cat knows better than to turn down a good meal.

"Good morning, puss," the female said. "Did you sleep well?"

The cat butted the female's leg with its head and smiled.

The cat felt strong this morning, but a cat always feels better after a warm sleep and a belly full of food. The female of the tall folk started dusting the small parlor, humming a jaunty tune as she worked. The cat watched for a moment, then it padded away, ready to explore the quiet corners and long hallways that filled the old house. It tiptoed along the sideboards filled with dusty bric-à-brac, pressed its whiskers against the gaps in the wills and the creaking skirting boards. It found the house's nooks and crannies, stalked the mice that lived in the pantry, and it chased the spots of sunlight that crept through the heavy curtains. It jumped on the bookcases and slept in the hazy, warm spots left by the sun. And everywhere it went, the cat could taste the passage of ghosts. The taste of them lingered in the air, making whiskers quiver with every unfamiliar scent. Dozens of ghosts, hundreds of ghosts, more than it could count. All of them lingering in the shadows and waiting until nightfall.

That evening the cat dined on mouse flesh, ripping apart a squeaker she'd caught by the cellar door. She could hear the wind rippling across the lawn, the quiet grumble of the ghosts in the walls, the lonely squall of the gramophone playing in the female's room. The cat followed the smell of the Female's sadness until it found her lying in bed, all wrapped up in her grandmother's pajamas while she listened to old records.

"Hello puss," the female said. "Still here are you?"

The cat leapt onto the bed. Butted her head against the female's leg until there were scratches behind the ears.

"I guess you can stay another night," the female said. "But you'd better leave in the morning. This isn't a good place for cats, you know. I thought it might have been this morning, but now…"

The cat nestled in next to the female while the gramophone wound down, was still there an hour later when the female fell asleep. The ghosts crept into the room in dribs and drabs, gathering around the female and preparing to feed. The cat kept its eyes closed, attention focused on the dusty smell of ghost as they filled the room. It could feel the ghost's presence in its whiskers and its bones, taste their very presence on the air.

"You should leave," the cat said. It spoke without opening its eyes. "This bed is my bed now, and this female is mine as well. Things will go badly if you try to take her back."

"We could take her," the tallest of the ghosts said. "We could take her back and eat you while we were at it. I hear cats are good eating if you prepare them right."

The ghost had a hideous smile on its face. The other ghosts chortled and cackled with glee.

"We could bundle you up in a sack," said the ghost with vacant eyes. "Bundle you up in a sack and drop you out a window. Watch you squiggle and squirm until you hit the ground below."

The cat didn't open its eyes, just flicked its tail and waited.

"Or we could just take what you've given her," the spectacled ghost said. "We can take all the dreams and the memories of you being here. We could make you cease to exist, little kitten, little cat. We could make you but another thing she misses in the night."

"It will not work," the cat said. "Anything she feels for me is mine, and nobody can steal anything that a cat possesses."

"You are just a cat," the tallest of the ghosts said. "A feeble cat that almost died in the wet of the storm. What can you do to stop us?"

"Well," said the cat. "I could start by doing this."

And with that, the cat lunged forward, both claws reaching out as though snaring a mouse. They dug into the ethereal wisp of the ghost's form, pinning him to the floor with eight sharp needles. The ghost struggled, unable to pull free, for a ghost is a shred of memories and longing; it had no strength of its own. The cat pulled its claws together and opened its hungry maw. The tallest ghost shrieked and gibbered, while the cat pinned the tattered scrap of its essence to the floor.

"How can you do this?" the tallest ghost wailed. "How can you touch me?"

"I am a cat," the cat whispered. "To a cat, there is nothing that can truly be forbidden."

Then it bared pale fangs in a wide smile and devoured the ghost, lapping the milky form with its tongue. With each silent lick, the ghost shrunk, growing smaller and smaller until he was little more than a pale dot against the darkness. His deep squeals and gibbering wails turned into the high-pitched squeal of a mosquito, until the cat ended them with a final dab and licked its lips. It was bigger now, and plumper, and there was something pleasant about the taste of ghost in its stomach.

Panic rippled through the ghosts around the bedchamber, a thrill of fear that sent shivers down the memory of what a spine should be.

"What have you done?" cried the ghosts. "How can a tiny cat eat a ghost, the largest of us all?"

The cat sat on the bedcovers, carefully licking its forepaw with a pale tongue. It cleaned the lingering taste of the tallest ghost of its whiskers, stroking them with a touch like velvet.

"I think you're all asking the wrong question," the cat said, calmly preening. "The question you should ask is *dear cat, oh dear cat, tell us honestly, please. Are you still hungry for ghost-flesh? Are you planning on eating me?*"

"Are you?" the ghosts cried. "Do you still hunger?"

The cat stood up, stretched its legs, and offered the collected ghosts a broad smile.

"My dear ghosts," the cat said . "I am simply starving."

It pounced, catching the ghost with vacant eyes and devouring him with three quick snaps of its jaws.

The ghosts gibbered and scattered, and the cat stalked and hunted, following the pale forms to their hidey-holes and shadowy perches. It hunted, and it feasted, devouring the ghosts one by one, until the only thing that moved in the house was the quiet rise and fall of the sleeping female's chest.

The last ghost it ate wore glasses, the smartest of its kind. It didn't wail or gibber, just accepted its fate with quiet calm. "I knew a cat would be trouble," it said in a buzzing voice. Then the cat licked it twice, and the ghost was gone.

The cat was fat and happy. It climbed onto the female's bed and breathed stolen memories over her face until dawn crept up on them.

That night the female had bad dreams and pleasant dreams and strange dreams beside. She remembered everything the ghosts had taken, all the memories of her grandmother and the house and her life. She woke up feeling happy, full of the past and the present and the possibility of a future. When she went downstairs, the cat was standing at the threshold, peering at the doorway with its great golden eyes. The female of the talk folk opened the door and sat on the steps, pressed a knuckle to her lips as she watched the cat climb down.

"Where are you going?" the female asked. "You could stay, if you wanted."

"I'm going in search of sunlight," the cat told her. "A warm patch of grass, the hum of the grasshoppers, and a shaded place to sleep. It's morning now, and I've had a long night. I need some time to rest."

"Will you be back?" the female asked, but the cat was already moving. Its black shape flitted down the stairwell, tail bob-bobbing as it leapt from step to step.

"I'll be back when the shadows are long," it called. "When the night is dark and the ghosts are strongest. I shall return when you need me, or when I wish it, or not at all. I'm a cat, I go where I please, and where I am needed, more often than not."

Then the cat was gone, disappearing into the long grass, rustling through the weeds and broken fences in search of a place to rest.

And the female of the tall folk never had trouble with ghosts again.

Elmshadow lowered his head and wheezed, drawing in a deep breath. The log burning in the fire cracked and threw sparks into the air, some of them landing just by Moonbelly's exposed stomach.

Moonbelly didn't flinch. "I liked it," she said. "It had mice."

Nobody responded. All eyes turned to the flame.

"I saw a ghost once," Foglick said, breaking the silence.

"Did you eat it?" Moonbelly's whiskers rippled as she twisted, scratching her back on the grass. "I hear they're good eating."

"It was sleeping on a couch in a tall-folks' house," Foglick said. He didn't offer any further explanation, and nobody asked him what he was doing in a tall-folk home. The stray prided himself on surviving in the wild, but there were still places a stray could find shelter if the cold was sharp enough.

"We've got time for another story," Elmshadow said. "Foglick seemed keen when I arrived, and we could do with something short."

Foglick flattened his ears and stared. He didn't speak up.

Starwalker rose and stretched out, front paws first, and then the back. "I'm not sure there's anywhere to go after ghosts," he said, and Moonbelly murmured her agreement. Skitterclaw seemed crestfallen, but Daffodil was hunting moths again, her attention already straying.

Foglick, sullen and slit-eyed on his perch atop the rock, didn't dare offer his thoughts.

"We should find something to eat," Elmshadow said. "There's not much night left, and this fires nearly done. I hear there are plump mice in the next field over. Maybe some grasshoppers, if one's up for a challenge."

Daffodil was off and bouncing, and Skitterclaw reluctantly followed. They disappeared into the long grass, rustling through the field by the woods.

Foglick roused himself. "There's a snow coming. I can taste it."

"Perhaps," Elmshadow said.

"We should eat before it hits." Foglick loped to the trees, where he paused and looked back at Elmshadow. "I'll give you this: the story left me hungry."

"Now you know how I feel," Moonbelly said.

"Your belly gets filled," Foglick said, and disappeared.

On the far side of the clearing, Elmshadow and Starwalker stood shoulder to shoulder. They watched Foglick's departure with solemn eyes, and Moonbelly knew they wanted her to leave as well. She acknowledged them both with a flick of her ears and ghosted her way into the trees. Not too far, and not too fast—she could move quietly when the spirit took her, and hide better than many suspected. She went up a tree and took refuge in the branches, looking back to watch the elder cats still seated by the fire.

Elmshadow closed one eye and slumped on the grass, close to the flame. His rear leg stuck out at an awkward angle as he lay there, stiff and unbending.

"Foglick will be trouble, eventually," Starwalker said.

"He's young," Elmshadow said. "He still has time to learn."

"The younglings might not survive that long."

"You cannot protect them." Elmshadow drew another long breath. His flank rose and fell with the effort. "Kittens grow up into cats, whether we like it or not. They'll learn to handle him with time."

Starwalker prowled the length of the clearing, tail lashing in irritation. "You could have told them what really happened, you know," Starwalker said. "They might fight ghosts, one day, and they'll need to know how."

"They'll learn that too, as you did, and as I did," Elmshadow said. "What it's like, and what it costs."

Starwalker walked the circle three times, then sat. "How many lives do you have left?"

Elmshadow laid his head across his paws and stared at Starwalker with his good eye. "You should hunt," he said. "And I should sleep. It was a long walk to get here, and there's a longer one coming to get home."

Starwalker cocked his head to one side and the crisp breeze tugged at his whiskers. For a moment, Moonbelly feared he would leave, but the piebald cat lay down and rested his head on Elmshadow's flank. The fire cracked again, dying but still warm, as they both settled into a drowsy sleep.

Nothing solved, then, but she was satisfied that the elder cats were thinking of the problem. She might do more, the next time the fire was lit, to ease the burden they shared.

Moonbelly crawled off the branch and disappeared into the woods. She could feel the others hunting out there, moving through the grass with delicate grace, launching themselves at humming grasshoppers desperate to escape. Her stomach rumbled, and the thought of grasshopper appealed, even if she'd rather a mouse or a rat, something with a little more fight to it.

She left the elder cats to the fire and slumber, and went out to join the hunt.

THE FINAL SEASON

Peeling off her gloves for extra traction, Maya glared at the Cee-Bee's mechanical leg and the stubborn lug nut that refused to move. She grabbed the wrench as long as her arm and leveraged it into place, threw her weight against it and pushed with all she had. Nothing. Well, almost nothing. Spending the day on hydraulics and servos instead of software hardly felt like one of her smarter decisions. Her bare hands ached with the cold of the garage, even with the heat lamps running. The pain mingled wlth the stew of frustration of anger that chased her in here, and she realized there'd be no solace in getting the big mech up and running again. Cee-Bee was a hunk of junk salvage job, mismatched parts cobbled together using parts from the scrapyard on the far side of Sinclair's Landing. Most days, working on him provided Maya with an escape from her father's *lets-terraform-Javal* bullshit, but those days didn't start with the news he'd hocked her mom's guitar in order to fund the next campaign.

"Fucker," Maya said, and it helped a little. She drew a long breath and tried to rein in the roiling emotions in her chest. She tapped the wrench against the stubborn leg, putting a little force behind it. Hitting something helped almost as much as swearing. The anger blasted forth, hot as a reactor link. "Frost-damned-idiot-fucking-useless-snow-blind-asshole-mother—"

"Hey!" Strong hands muscled her away from Cee-Bee's leg. Maya attempted to kick free, half-blind with the rush of anger, but powerful arms held her tight until the anger ebbed away. Worse, the tears leaked out anyway. Dammit.

"It's okay," she said. "I'm okay."

Alexander O'Day cinched the hug tighter. "Sure, you've having a great day."

Sarcasm. Close to a good sign—it meant Alex was worried, but wasn't fretting about saying the wrong thing. Maya sucked in a calming breath. "You can let me go. It's done."

Alex released her grip and retreated a few short steps, concern writ across face. Maya met that concern with a frustrated scowl, her jaw hard and her whole body tensed for a fight. Alex had a good six inches on her, powerful arms and the kind of reflexes that meant she was destined for a bright future as a corporate pilot rather than a Javali mech jockey. Any fight would be short and unpleasant for Maya, but Alex rarely rose to the bait. She merely raised an eyebrow and raised the hand still holding the wrench she'd wrestled away. "Might want me to be unarmed before you take a swing, yeah?"

The tension evaporated and Maya's shoulders sagged, anger dissolving into a flurry of nervous laughter. Maya let the relief of it pull her to the workshop's taped-up chair, and she flopped into it with far more drama than dignity. "Didn't hear you come in," she said.

"No surprise. Beating on Cee-Bee makes a hell of a racket." Alex tapped the wrench against her thigh, customary smile reasserting itself now the danger had passed. "You want to talk about what sent you all psycho-killer?"

"No."

"Then let's start with the simple stuff," Alex said. "What's wrong with Ceeb?"

"Everything."

"What's your big three, then?"

Maya huffed out a sigh. "Latest update to his code introduced static on the neural link. The aft lower exhaust isn't operating at full capacity, and the stupid leg casing won't come off. Lug nuts are screwed in tight, and the right leg is still seizing up on corners."

"Right-o." Alex slid the wrench into place with a single movement, setting her shoulders against the tension. Broad shoulders bunched beneath her jacket, a prelude to the pressure she exerted against the stubborn nut. She grunted with satisfaction when the effort resulted in movement. Alex grinned and leveraged her weight beneath the wrench, pushing until the lug nut gave up. "One down," she said. "You want to work, or you want to tell me why Ceeb needed to cop a beating?"

"Work," Maya said. "You pick the tunes."

Alex accessed the stream and selected an old Green Day album, all driving bass and snarling guitar with a little pop mixed in. Not Maya's first choice, but Alex hadn't really grown up with a mother obsessed with pre-warp classics. The O'Days were Javal's old money, the family who sponsored the first colony landing and owned two-thirds of the planet. While Maya learned the chords to Anarchy in the UK on her mother's knee, Alex learned to lie low during the O'Day family's lengthy verbal battles. Anger wasn't her favorite emotion, even if she had a right to unleash an avalanche of rage when her family was concerned.

"Good choice," Maya said, and Alex beamed at the compliment.

"Get what you need, babe. I'll get us access to Cee-Bee's innards."

Maya gathered cables while Alex removed the rest of the casing, lost herself in the wordless focus of hooking up the diagnostic computer to the Mech's internal systems. The initial scan showed a glitch in the servo-regulators, and a visual inspection confirmed the flaw—easily fixed with a little TLC and bodged-together parts. Alex played assistant while Maya climbed up Cee-Bee's foot to get a better angle on the defective part. Slowly, the cold core of anger thawed, warmed by the pleasure of Alex's presence and the joy of inching Cee-Bee closer to being race-ready.

The admission came without preamble: "Dad sold Mum's Stratocaster."

Alex met the news with a low whistle of acknowledgment, but she didn't push for details. Maya unscrewed the regulator, handed off each one to Alex for safekeeping. "Hocked it to your granddad's store, hoping to get together enough credit to broadcast adds through all five settlements. Stupid burn-case thinks we're going to rise up and demand they rebuild the planet into something a little more habitable."

"Your dad dreams big," Alex said.

"He's an idiot."

"Not a mutually exclusive state of affairs," Alex said.

"It wasn't *his*," Maya said. "Mom left the Strat to me."

"And on that, you have my sympathy, but it ain't like beating on Cee-Bee here is going to get the guitar out of hock."

Maya deployed a withering look, and Alex met it with a cheeky grin. "We'll need a better plan, I think. Something folks will pay for, maybe."

"I have a plan." Maya handed the last screw off and unclipped the regulator from its casing. She slid it free with a grunt, used both hands to lug it over to the workbench and her tools. "I'm entering Cee-Bee into the circuit, and we're going to walk away with this year's prize money."

"Oh." Alex's grin disappeared in an instant, and her forehead creased. "Are you sure?"

"First choice was hacking dad's accounts, but he's already spent the credits," Maya said. "Can't think of much else that will get me what I need before the guitar's sent off-world."

Alex chewed her lower lip. "You might want something a little more certain. Low-risk."

"You don't think Cee-Bee can do it?"

Alex gazed up at the big, mismatched robot. "Can't say he'll be the favorite."

"Cee-Bee ain't much to look at, but he can move when I need him to and the interface is solid. And there's nobody on this hunk of ice who can build a mech half as good on a budget, yeah? All I need's a gun pilot attached to the trodes…"

Alex took a deep interest in her hands. "Academy messaged yesterday," she said. "I fly out in three weeks to start my first semester."

The news suckerpunched Maya in the gut. "Shit. "I mean, that's awesome, but—"

"That's not the issue," Alex said. "The family went nuts. Mom and Dad got into a fight with Granddad, and he's gone overboard about his firstborn granddaughter working off planet."

"Your grandpa's an ass."

"He is," Alex said. "He's insisting I prove myself before I can go. Wants me on the circuit… with Ruby-Go-Go."

Maya pushed back the goggles. "You're leaving?"

"Day after the last race," Alex said.

"You're *racing* and you're leaving?"

"It's not like I'm itching to do one last drift. Granddad insists. Family pride and all that. My family has to deal with the asshole after I'm gone, and you know he'll be unbearable—"

For the second time that night, Maya could feel tears brimming, ready to spill. For the second time, she decided anger was preferable to the ache of loss. "Get out."

"Come on, Maya. It's just—"

"GET OUT!"

Alex retreated two steps, both hands raised in surrender. "I gotta do it, May. You know what the old man's like when shiz don't go his way."

She did. Maya knew about the fights, the shouting matches that sent Alexander into the snow, searching for refuge in the beat-up workshop owned by the local crackpot. The insistence that Alex stay on Javal, big fish in a small pond. Take over the family business, run Sinclair's Landing for the benefit of the family.

Maya knew all that, and she didn't care. It hurt too much to care. She stomped the feelings down, compacted them into a cold, dark shiv of raw anger, ready to lash out. Tonight could fucking suck it.

"Guess I'll see you on the ice," she said.

"May, come on. I wanted—"

"We're done here, Lex," Maya said. "Thanks for your help removing the casing, but I don't got much time to get Cee-Bee race-ready and you're technically the competition now."

Alex lingered, weight shifting from foot to foot, eager to find some words that might break the wall of ice. Maya tapped into the stream and changed the music over to Stiff Little Fingers, one of her mother's favorite bands. And one band Alex had never really jibed with, even after the musical education she'd received in the workshop.

Maya tapped the volume up a few levels and turned back to Cee-Bee's innards. She barely heard Alex's departure over the angry squall of her playlist.

Maya spent two straight days repairing Cee-Bee, and another three clearing up the issues with his software and calibrating the trodes to eke out a better performance when it mattered.

At sixteen, the circuit still required parental permission before they'd let her race, but Maya had long-ago hacked her father's console and rigged a back door. Ten minutes of data entry, and she'd officially registered as Number Eight and tasked a workshop drone with branding Cee-Bee's paint job with the number.

Ten days in total since the fight, and she'd still heard nothing from Alex. Maya contemplated calling, a way to break the silence. Then she'd remember Alex was leaving—and screwing her over on the way out—and the anger festering in her stomach grew cold and sharp once more. Nothing mattered but winning, and she didn't even need the entire circuit. The purse from one race could buy-back the Stratocaster, particularly one of the local legs where competition would be fierce and Maya could make a few bucks betting on the side.

On the sixth day, her father launched a new campaign pushing for terraforming, the small living room of their quarters filled with screens as he gathered the brain's trust to fine-tune the new message. Long-winded, earnest speeches from the most boring members of every settlement on Javal, with her father the worst of the lot. Maya endured the waffling for the better part of an hour, thought better of listening to more. She left a note on the household stream and layered up to walk the streets, trudging through the snow-covered town as night fell.

Sinclair's Landing was a make-your-own-fun kind of town, and cold enough after dark that most people elected to manufacture whatever amusements they conceived inside and at home, behind their insulated walls and the heat lamps fending off the worst of the planet's frigid squalls. Maya had the street to herself as she walked, pushing through the low drifts that filled the streets.

She hadn't meant to find her way to Halcyon Antiques and Pawn Shop, but her feet found the place without being asked and Maya stood before the frost-rimmed glass, looking in on the cluttered landscape of old chairs, faded paintings, ancient tech, and other detritus that colonies brought to Javal with the limited weight allowance devoted to personal affects. Her mother's Strat hung on the far wall, cherry red curves marked and scored with decades of heavy use, and Maya could still hear her mother's raspy snarl as she played ancient punk songs about being pretty and vacant.

Maya's fingers knew the weight of the guitar, the pressure required to create a chord and coax snarling music out of its strings. The protective callouses were long gone now—it felt sacrilegious to touch the Stratocaster after mom passed—but the joy of Mom's beloved punk songs were the easy, three-chord rhythms. "It's all about the attitude," Mom always said, then she'd launch into an ancient Sex Pistols tune about being so pretty and so vacant.

They'd been dead three hundred years, so Maya knew The Sex Pistols were never trapped on a planet on the ass-end of nowhere. Still, she figured they knew a little about what it was like. It was right there in the leering, strutting anger of their song. The hurt, the anger, a future filled with going nowhere fast.

Alex was getting out, though.

The traitorous thought brought a fresh pang of anger. Nobody but Alex was winning the circuit this year. For all the time Alex O'Day spent lurking around Maya's workshop, her own rig was a state-of-the-art mech built for sprinting across the ice. Ruby-Go-Go had been responsible for more race wins on Javal than anyone, racking up five in as many years. Nobody knew how much it cost to import the crimson beast, nor why Old Man O'Day thought it necessary to dominate the races, but he invested heavily in the project. While everyone else drove work mechs doubling as racing machines, or cobbled together rigs forged from spare parts like Cee-Bee, Ruby didn't leave the O'Day's workshop for anything but racing.

The advantage Ruby-Go-Go provided would have been galling if Alex hadn't been so damn good, capable of beating the pants of anyone regardless of what she drove. In a junker like Cee-Bee, with all Maya's tweaks, she would have been the odds-on favorite. Once she climbed into Ruby-Go-Go's cockpit, Alex O'Day became unbeatable on the track. She had the speed, the connection, and the skill to slide into the corners and pick up speed after.

The only way Alex and Ruby went down is if something *took* them down from the inside, and there were damn few people the O'Day's trusted enough to get close enough for that.

Alex trusted Maya, though. Half the things she'd learned about racing came from watching her friend practice, both on the track and in the virtual rigs in the O'Day hanger.

Maya wrote the virus in twelve adrenaline-fueled hours, holing up in the hanger with Cee-Bee's looming presence and the Buzzcocks' two-guitar assault turned up to full volume. She needed the anger of the music to calm the roil of guilt in her stomach, and even then she stopped three times to remind herself that Alex would be fine. Losing the race wasn't the end of the world for her. *Alex* always had options. Maya was the one who'd be stuck here, nose pressed to the pawnshop window until the Strat finally disappeared, and after that, she had what?

Her dad? A future spent mining ice to ship off-world for the orbital colonies? Screw that. She needed the money way more than Alex did.

There were security guards out front of the O'Day family hanger when she fronted up there the following morning, but she recognized them both. The skinny one, Gallo, had been working for the O'Days for the last three years, while the shorter, plumper Denny Chen had been working for family nigh on a decade. They both nodded a greeting as Maya approached, but Chen's expression was hang-dog and worried. Sinclair's Landing wasn't large enough for a fight with Alex go to unnoticed, even with the handful of visitors coming in to cover the race.

"Been a while since we saw you around here," Chen said.

"Been a while since I had something to say." Dana shuffled in place, gaze dropping to the crust of snow at her feet. "Alex in?"

"Due for a practice run in thirty," Chen said. "Want us to tell her you're waiting?"

Maya huffed warm air into her palms. "Nah, too cold to stand around in snow."

"Warm inside," Chen said. "And I know she'd love to see you."

Johnny Rotten bless small towns and the urge to interfere. Maya bit her lip, making a show of indecision. She hurried both hands in the pockets of her jacket and looked away, offered a sheepish nod. Chen beamed at her and swiped her visitor pass, pointing towards the second door doorway. "They're running training sims today. Best chance to catch her without the old man about is up on the mezzanine."

Maya could work with that. "Thanks, Denny."

"No problem. Just make up with her, yeah? I got money on the race this year, and she doesn't race good when you're pissed at her."

"Maybe she's pissed at me," Maya said, and it drew a snort of laughter from Gallo. Nobody ever believed the golden girl of the O'Days got mad at anything, not when the misfit kid who listened to the Misfits was right there being pissed at everything. That was okay. Maya knew what folks thought of her family, and why they thought it. She made a beeline for the doorway, swiped her card and divested herself of thermal jackets on the far side.

Every time she walked into the O'Day family hangar, it was like stepping into another world. Three times the size of her cramped workspace, with three tiered mezzanines allowing access to every part of Ruby-Go-Go and the three other mechs the family owned. Built-in computers banks with the power to pilot a starship instead of shitty handhelds, tools mounted on the walls instead of stacked in heaps and piles. The stark, clinical efficiency of the place grated against her nerves, but it never failed to showcase the advantage Alex held over every other racer.

Fuck knows why she kept coming over to Maya's place, tooling around on Cee-Bee and helping Maya scavenge parts from the scrapyard. Maya settled in with her hand terminal, feigning the air of a girl waiting in the warmth instead of engaging in skulduggery. Her terminal logged onto the local network, the security codes installed on her first visit and re-used every time she came. It didn't allow immediate access to Ruby-Go-Go's systems, but it wasn't hard to create a backdoor access and slip her virus into the operating systems. The whole thing was over in ten minutes, tops, and Ruby would go out there with a Trojan horse waiting Dana's signal.

Dana sighed and packed her terminal away, gazed up at the sleek lines of Ruby's chassis. They'd exposed the top of the hanger to the air, easier to lift the big robot out when it was time to take her on a run, and frost rimed the head and shoulders that dwarfed every other mech on the circuit. It would have been a dream to race her, an even bigger dream to beat Ruby-Go-Go legit, but stack decks favored the O'Days and there was no way to tip the scales while playing by the rules. Maya triggered a playlist and settled in, steeling herself for what came next. Rancid, followed by Stiff Little Fingers. Two of her mother's favorites.

"Dana!" The relief in Alex's voice caught Dana by surprise. Her friend rushed across the mezzanine and scooped Dana in a tight hug, the puffy sleeves of her jacket still damp as the ice melted in the hanger's warmth. "It's good to see you," Alex said. "I'm sorry about… shit, you know, everything."

Movement by the door caught Dana's attention. Riordan O'Day, Dana's grandfather, scowled at Dana as he shucked off his jacket and hung it by the door. Dana scowled right back at him, focusing her anger on the old man so it didn't seep into her voice.

"It's okay," she said. "I know you've got no choice. Doesn't mean I won't kick your ass the moment we're on the ice."

Riordan O'Day raised his nose and sniffed, loudly. A pointed reminder he didn't approve of his granddaughter's friendship. "We've got a schedule," he said, voice like something emerging from a tomb.

"Screw the schedule," Alex said. "It can wait five minutes."

"I'm afraid it can't," Riordan said. "I've got another appointment. You've got practice."

Alex's eyes filled with an apology, and Dana accepted with a nod. "Go do your run," she said. "I'll see you at the race."

"May the best mech win," Alex said.

Dana smiled. "It will."

The days before the race were always busy, even when Dana wasn't racing. Outsiders came to Sinclair's Landing in the lead-up to first circuit, arriving in pairs or small groups. The shuttle port on the far side of the ridge spent almost as much time porting people as ice, and the handful of bars and hotels around the town filled to the brim with off-worlders who arrive with shiny new jackets and drone cameras, complaining bout the bitter cold in their strange accents.

Maya's father spent those days campaigning with his Terraformer buddies, making it known Javal wasn't content to provide ice to the rest of the sector. The people indentured there deserved a real life, on a planet capable of more than months of endless winter. Maya barely saw him, outside of his hurried return to the house to pick up supplies, and she divided her time between getting Cee-Bee race worthy and fretting about the possibility that some off-worlder would pick up the Strat. Every evening, just before the worst of the cold truly set in, she'd do the same circuit: twenty minutes downtown to watch the guitar through the Halcyon Antiques and Pawn Shop Window. Twenty-three minutes over to the perimeter of the O'Day hanger, hanging back in the shadows and confirmed her virus had given her a backdoor into Ruby-Go-Go's systems and hadn't been discovered. Another thirty-three minutes to get home, where she'd retreat into the hanger and work on Cee-Bee-Gee-Bee until the wee hours.

She might have Ruby-Go-Go covered, but there were still other mechs in the race and plenty of contenders who could provide a challenge. The blissful hours spent refining the mech's code and fine-tuning the salvaged parts almost distracted her from the gnawing guilt that followed every message Alex sent over the networks.

Dana was engrossed in fixing the Cee-Bee's knee joint when Riordan O'Day visited the hanger. Riordan's grandfather pressed the buzzer by the doorway, startling the ancient intercom system to life for the first team in over a year. His long face peered up at the camera overhead, gaunt and disproving, and he wore a thin coat loaded with thermal patches rather than the puffy jackets favored by the bulk of Javal's citizens. Dana pushed back her goggled and rested her wrench on one shoulder, unsure what the hell Riordan O'Day was doing in her neck of the woods, let alone knocking on her door. Part of her wondered if they'd discovered her backdoor code, but Riordan wouldn't front up personally for that. He'd gather his security goons and send them out to collect her, drag Dana into his home turf for the interrogation and threat of retaliation.

Riordan thumbed the buzzer a second time, the irritated creases of his expression blooming into an outright scowl. Dana swore and hustled over to open the door, raking one hand through her lank hair. "Mister O'Day, I—"

"This?"

The contempt in Riordan O'Day's voice put Dana on the back foot, and he pushed past her and surveyed the cramped clutter of Dana's workspace with an expression of outright disgust. "So this is what my granddaughter believes is more important than her legacy here."

Dana blinked at the old man's back. "Sir?"

"Close the door, girl." Riordan O'Day made a beeline for Cee-Bee, dodging past the scattered parts. "I doubt you've got the money to burn heating this place, and this will already take longer than I'd like."

Fuck you, Dana thought. Her mother's favored response, full of punk-rock energy and outright rebellion against men like Riordan O'Day and his assumed place at the top of the pile. But the old man had a point, and Dana sealed them inside the hanger's warmth, checking the seals for the first time in years rather than simply slamming the portal shut and trusting things would hold. O'Day was already on the far side of the room, studying the interface code scrolling across Maya's terminal screen.

"This is good work," he said. "Inelegant, and crude, but you've definitely got a knack for this. I can see why my granddaughter speaks highly of you, even if your father's an idiot with no understanding of what he asks for."

"I'm not my father," Dana said.

"No. I suspect you take after your mother, which suggests you'd be smarter than him by far." O'Day jerked his chin at the Cee-Bee's right knee. "You've rebuilt this out of an old B-12 limb?"

"Mixed in some parts from a Pennington Gen 4," Dana said.

"The B-12 wasn't the most reliable model. Knee joints gave out under pressure. It's why we stopped using them to mine."

"I've got it covered," Dana said. "Reinforced the struts, and the weight distribution is different. Gives the whole mech better balance, even if he weighs a little heavy on the turns."

"And there's compensation built into your code?"

"Seemed like a kindness to whoever piloted the mech. Wouldn't want them walking with a limp just cause Cee-Bee's off-kilter."

O'Day grunted and rose to his full height, casting about for a place to sit. He was out of luck—spare parts occupied every flat surface in the hanger, and Dana wasn't about to pull out the folding chairs to entertain him. "Did you want something, sir?"

"My granddaughter," the old man said, "has a great deal of affection for you. I've never approved of it, or understood it, but I've permitted your friendship so far as it doesn't affect Alexander's future or curb her potential."

Dana bristled at the suggestion. "Last I heard, she was heading for the academy after this year's race."

"Which isn't a future any O'Day should aspire to, but it's more ambition than her father had." O'Day rubbed a thumb against the pads of his fingers, as though trying to clear a smear of dirt. He'd touched nothing since entering the room, and wore gloves when pressing the buzzer. "Still, there's no denying the girl has a gift, and she's shown none of the head for business that would have made her content to stay on Javal. Better this than no ambitions at all."

"If you say so, sir."

"I do." Riordan O'Day "I'm not an unreasonable man, Miss Halpern. I know Alexander offered to pilot your mech this season, and while you've made an impressive machine with the parts you had available—"

"I'm sorry," Dana said. "Alex offered to do *what*?"

Riordan O'Day's reasonable façade gave way to the stern, patrician anger. "Don't play coy with me, girl. Alexander confronted me with your offer, swore the only way she wanted to race this year is piloting this ramshackle beast you've pulled together from junk. She claims it's the only fair way to showcase she's truly the best pilot this planet has."

"I never asked her to do that," Dana said.

Riordan O'Day was inured to her sally. "Then you will not be disappointed to learn there's no chance in hell it's happening. We have already committed Alexander to the race as the pilot of the O'Day family mech, and that will not be changing. However—" he raised a finger to stall Dana's objections "—I will concede she's at least partially right about your talents, Miss Halpern. What you've achieved her with very little is impressive, and I'd be curious to see how your talents play out when given more resources."

"I suppose you're offering me a job," Dana said, grinning at the absurdity of it.

"Yes," O'Day said, and Dana's grin froze. "Junior mechanic, learning the ropes under my senior staff. You'll service our working mechs, plus my granddaughter's racing model. Her youngest cousin will take over as pilot in the next season, and they'll not have Alexander's feel for the machine. Access to a coder with your mechanical instincts could be useful for us, and if you've half the gifts Alexander claims, I suspect you'll be running my hanger within a few years."

Riordan O'Day swept both hands behind his back, affecting a dignified interest in Cee-Bee's piton sling rig rather than waiting for an answer. In his world, people didn't say no very often, least of all a backyard mechanic who'd been clinging to his granddaughter's coattails for a decade. Dana's blood surged, riding a wave of anger, although she didn't allow it to show on her face.

"With all due respect," she said. "Go to hell."

Surprise washed across O'Day's face, and Dana knew where it was coming from. She could scarce believe she'd said the words, let alone given them sufficient vehemence to actually stall the old man.

"This is an opportunity rarely offered to locals," O'Day said.

"No shit. And for the record, fuck right off with your shit as well." Dana drew a deep breath, tracking the twitch in O'Day's jaw as he fought with his anger. "You came in here to accuse me of trying to poach Alex as a pilot, which is so much bullshit it's actually laughable. I *have* a pilot for Cee-Bee, and we don't plan on making it easy for Alex to walk away the winner. If your granddaughter is giving you grief about not wanting to race, maybe it's because she doesn't want to race anymore?"

"What she wants is of minimal importance here," O'Day said. "She's still a girl. A girl with talent and potential, but young people are foolish with both. Her future is bright—"

"And that's great for her, but she's not the only with a lifetime in front of her here. I'd rather stake my future on my own skills and the mech I pulled together than accept a handout from a condescending ass like you."

Riordan O'Day peered at her with an expression of faint distaste, his lip curled around some retort he never vocalized. The anger in the tall man should have been intimidating, but Dana's own anger kept her standing resolute, staring him down. She was already better than any engineer Riordan O'Day had on his staff, as evidenced by the ease with which she'd slipped a virus into his mechs's systems.

But it hurt that this man was so important in her friend's life and held so much sway in Alexander O'Day's decisions.

"Now that we've ascertained I'm not stealing your pilot, and I have no interest in working for you, I think it's time you left," Dana said. "Race day is coming sooner than either of us would like, and I've got a lot of preparation to do before I put my mech on the line."

They stared at one another, neither willing to move, but it was Dana's hanger and Dana's mech, and O'Day was the intruder. He held the line as long as he dared, making it clear he wasn't backing down, but ultimately he was the one to nod and excuse himself, collecting his jacket and disappearing into the frosty night.

The invitational circuit was Javal's second-biggest export, after ice, and it probably earned more money than anything else that occurred on-planet. The verse was a big, slightly boring place, and the harsh conditions, graceful skill, and spectacular fuck-ups that accompanied big mechs racing over ice proved to be a cult hit. Maya had never really figured out what that meant, but it probably accounted to one or two fans on whatever station, colony, or capital ship humanity occupied. Unimpressive numbers in isolation, but the human diaspora covered countless worlds, and the small handfuls here and there quickly added up.

Pity none of the racers who risked their lives on the circuit ever really got to see a damn thing other than Javal's ice and snow, but the other half of "cult hit" seemed to involve doing things on the cheap. Kludged-together mechs, amateur racers, a handful of drones to capture race footage and edit it together. Maybe one racer in a generation made it out of Javal's gravity, and everybody knew Alexandra O'Day was this generation's star.

Maya pushed that thought aside, along with the surge of jealousy that came hot on its heels. She triggered the final diagnostics on her terminal, then brought up the map of today's course. There were Thirty-two mechs lined up for the first race, and opening leg of the circuit aimed to eliminate those who would not measure up for the rest of the season. Twenty-three kilometers of slick ice and cross-country snow, 72 tight corners as the track snaked up the nearby mountains, then curved down to follow the bank where secure ice gave way to the fragile crust that covered Javal's churning seas.

The inexperienced assumed it was the mountain curves that got you. Fastest way to navigate the track was letting the mech's drift through a corner, retracting the traction spikes and letting six tons of steel skid across the ice, positioning yourself for a fast take-off when you hit the next straight. Plenty of racers went over the edge attempting the tight curves up-top, but a mech jockey could probably survive the fall if their machine went over.

What cost people their lives on the track was the curve near the sea—a tight hairpin where the line between safe ice and thin was easily missed, and the same six tons of mech would plunge through into the churning sea below. The last major curve before the straight run to the finish line. Locals called it the Saberstine Turn, named after the first man to die there. Recovering a mech from those depths would be difficult, even if they scrambled a rescue team in time. Even then, too much time spent in the frigid waters presented a very different round of problems.

Even Alex risked nothing fancy on the Saberstine. She went in slow and controlled, more focused on getting out alive than making up extra seconds. "If I haven't won a race by that corner," she always said, "nothing I do there's going to change anything."

Maya pushed the thought away and focused on the race map, imprinting the course on her mind, worrying at her lower lip.

The diagnostics finished their sweep, and there were no surprises there. Cee-Bee was in good shape for an old banger build, and her problems were all familiar and able to be worked around. Maya slid into the cockpit and strapped herself into the pilot's seat. They'd built the rig for Alex's lanky frame, but it had been an exercise in function rather than comfort. Maya lacked her friend's height, but it didn't avail her much extra room and the sweltering heat persisted, even with the frosty temperatures outside. Momentary pain for long-term gain, or at least that's what Maya told herself as she secured her feet, knees, and waist. She attached the gel-tipped trodes to her forehead and fired up the mech's OS. Virtual feeds blossomed over the physical controls, and the heavy weight of Cee-Bee's limbs settled over her. Maya flipped the overhead switches to fire up the engine, then activated the speakers. Fast-paced guitars burst to life as she went through the pre-race checks, testing each arm and leg to ensure they were responding to her movements. Overhead, the Ramones sang about being sedated, and Maya's adrenaline rose with the rapid-fire chant of 1-2-3-4 that began each song.

Cee-Bee's onboard computer reached out and tagged the other mechs in the race, each appearing on the mech's nav system, ready to be tracked. Alex and Ruby Go-Go were already on the line, crouched and ready to spring. No sign of nerves or preflight systems, just a precision machine with the best pilot on Javal, ready to go out and win. Maya's systems shook hands with Ruby's computer, slipped in the second half of the virus with nobody the wiser. All it would take is a simple activation trigger and there'd be a second-long lag in Ruby-Go-Go's responses, which meant all Maya and Cee-Bee needed to do was stay close enough to overtake them once the opportunity presented itself.

Maya sucked down a deep breath. The air in Cee-Bee's cockpit was already stiflingly warm. She satisfied herself that everything was hunky dory—the right leg felt stiff, but usable, and Maya hoped it would get through the race without issue. If that failed, there wasn't a virus in the world that could tip the balance in her favor.

She took the line and dropped into a crouch, spikes emerging from Cee-Bee's feet to give them traction on the ice. The other racers fell in, spreading through the empty space between Ruby's position and Cee-Bee's. Maya focused on breathing, letting herself fall into the moment. That was a trick Alex taught her: don't anticipate the starting gun, or you're liable to break ranks. Just let the moment be, ready to flow like the watery depths beneath Javal's frozen crust.

The comms lit up, a request from Alex in Ruby-Go-Go, one last confab before the race.

Maya turned up the volumes on the Ramones and focused on the moment: the press of the gimbaled crash-chair against her back, the musty smell of the cockpit with too little ventilation and too much proximity to the engines that kept Cee-Bee running; the forbidding red of the starter's lights, and the quiet cheer of the small community that turned out to watch the start of the race.

Maya slowed her thoughts and breathed, just like Alex had taught her.

Then the light went green, and everything became chaos and motion.

Maya burst out of the starting position, Cee-Bee's traction spikes operating perfectly and giving her a burst of speed. She pulled ahead going into the first turn, a gentle curve where the thick ice was perfect for a three-point drift, and Maya retracted her traction and dropped into position in a picture perfect routine. Cee-Bee slid across the thick ice, twisting as he went, then kicked in the spikes as she launched herself down the next straight. One by one, the other racers followed suit; Alex and Ruby right on Maya's heels, then the others.

The opening portion of the track was all quick bursts and short drifts, and one of the slower mechs—Aiden Moors, piloting Husky H—wiped out and fell into a snowbank three corners in. Steam rose from the crash site as Husky's engines burned through the ice, then cooled. Maya and Cee-Bee were already heading into the fourth, sharper and tighter, but the long straight coming out of it would take them two and a half clicks from town. No fans there, just the drones recording the race and broadcasting it across the feeds. Maya went into the slide, realized she'd overcompensated. Too much speed going in meant she'd overshoot her take-off point, cost herself a few precious seconds before she could risk putting down spikes and sprinting.

Alex and Ruby-Go-Go had no such issue. The crimson mech moved fluidly, dropping into the turn with one arm extended to support a deep lean. Coming out with preternatural balance, picking up speed down the straight. Ruby was light, built for these long straights and the speed she could make up on them. Maya kicked Cee-Bee into gear and went after her friend. She was dimly aware of the other five racers coming up in their wake, the closest of them Hannie Ray in Junker Joe, a kludged-together mech almost as ugly as Cee-Bee. They'd built Junker for the straights too, making up ground Hannie Ray lost on the curves, but Maya didn't sweat her.

This was a two woman race, as far as she was concerned, and there weren't many folks on Javal who could change Maya's mind.

The race was just six minutes old when they hit the mountains, Alex out in front and Maya running on her heels. Aiden Moors and Husky H were in the third place, trailing a half-minute behind the lead after a bad slide on the prior corner. Husky could corner well—better than most of the other racers—but Aiden wasn't a pilot who liked to push his luck. He'd take the mountain curves with care, probably willing to take the third place purse rather than crash out and lose the season.

Alex and Ruby-Go-Go didn't have that kind of trouble. They hit the first curve at speed, Alex killing the traction spikes and sliding the crimson mech right up to the edge before launching into the next stretch. There was an art to a good drift —a precision—starting with the outstretched hand that provided the pivot-point. The back leg provided the power, launched the mech like a sprinter down the next straight, but kicking into the sprint in a way that didn't fry your servos was always a problem. Alex did it better than anyone Maya had ever seen, and Ruby-Go-Go's legs could handle the torque that would snap Cee-Bee's leg at the knee.

It was beautiful to watch, even from the position right behind her, trying to manage her own slide into the corner and stay close enough to be a contender. Maya hit the corner at fifty clicks an hour, slower than she wanted but still plenty fast enough to feel the half-G pull of the velocity tugging at her. She kicked off and tore after Maya, picking up speed on the downward slope. The next three corners were a slalom race, sharp turns and short straights all the way to the bottom. Ruby-Go-Go owned this stretch, and Maya's radar tracked the seconds as Alex pulled ahead.

Then, on the third curve from the end, she caught a break— Alex mistimed the curve; her fear foot coming perilously close to the edge and a short tumble over the cliff. Ruby-Go-Go stumbled into the take-off, her left foot skidding as it should have gained traction on the next step. Alex recovered fast, straightening up and finding a new equilibrium as she lurched into a sprint, but it cost her precious seconds and allowed Maya to close the gap.

Pity her heart lurched in those precious moments when it seemed Alex might go over. She got Cee-Bee around the curve and thumbed her comms, sending a short-band Ruby-Go-Go's way. "You okay in there?"

"Fine." The word barked, blunt. No doubt fit in between the string of curses as Alex swore to herself.

Then the next straight was done, and Ruby-Go-Go went into the slide. Picture perfect, no mistakes. Making up lost seconds before they hit the straight.

Maya's radar tracked Alex's growing lead and she realized this was it. The logical place to trigger the virus in Ruby's system. With the early stumble, there'd be fewer questions if Alex wiped out on the final mountain curve. "Cee-Bee, you got that activation code?"

"Ready," the computer responded.

"Broadcast on my mark," Maya said.

Alex went into the last turn, sleek and fast and perfectly controlled. It was criminal to ruin it, guitar or no guitar.

To say nothing of the outrage the O'Day's would unleash, if they ever discovered what Maya had done. The anger that would flow from Alex herself, in that brief window where they still spoke.

She's leaving anyway. You'll never see her again.

Ruby-Go-Go's momentum shifted, preparing for the launch.

Now or never, Alex thought. Then she made the call: "Computer, cancel the code."

Ruby-Go-Go picked up traction on the ice, kicking up frost as the long legs churned. Alex launched herself into the straight, cursing herself as they headed for the Saberstine and the long, coastal run towards the end of the circuit.

The Saberstine Corner was the hardest drift of the race, a tight hairpin curve against the vast, ice-sheathed sea. Racers won and lost on the Saberstine, and accidents were most likely to happen there, when pilots didn't control their skid and slid a four-ton mech onto ice that couldn't bear its weight. Every mech had an automated eject system installed, ready to throw the pilot clear in the event the machine went under, and most days, it was enough.

Most days, but not today. Ruby Go-Go powered towards the Saberstine. The mech moved like a dream, arms pumping, exhaust vents steaming. Cee-Bee's sensors clocked her at 60 clicks an hour and picking up speed going into the turn.

A risky prospect, but Alex could handle it. Experience and natural reflexes gave her one heck of an edge, even without a beast like Ruby. Maya's attempts to keep pace were futile—she barely dared to clear fifty-two clicks an hour, and sue sure as heck wasn't trying to speed up. A small, controlled drift would net her second place. Fewer credits, but maybe she could talk Old Man O'Day into holding the Strat until she got the rest. Maybe—

Ruby Go-Go dropped into a three-point stance and slid into the corner, the big mech's bulk twisting to prepare for a new sprint. It looked picture perfect, but Cee-Bee's sensors screamed warnings. Alex had pushed the mech too fast, picked up enough speed to hit the outer bank and drift onto the ice.

Maya thumbed the radio, screaming out a warning, but tragedy hit before the words left her throat. Alex dropped Ruby's traction spikes, preparing to launch herself, and the thin ice cracked beneath the metal foot. Shattered beneath four tons of shifting weight, and dumped Ruby Go-Go into the frigid water beyond. Maya's heart surged. She dropped into her drift, Cee-Bee crouched low and ready to take the lead, surge down the two-click straight between her and sweet, sweet victory.

But Ruby's eject system didn't fire. As she went down, Alex went down along with her, trapped in the cockpit and destined to freeze the moment water seeped in.

The other three competitors were coming in fast, thundering towards the Saberstine and preparing to overtake. Maya swore and adjusted Cee-Bee's weight, jamming a steel hand into the ice. She slid to a halt beside the corner of the track, fifty clicks from the broken surface where Alex had gone under. She thumbed her radio to life. "Lex, hold on. I'm coming out."

The response was little more than static, the occasional word punctuating the fuzz. "…stuck…help…go…"

Maya flipped Cee-Bee's sensors and scanned the ice sheet for a safe path, unfurled the tether line on the mech's right arm and the magnetic grapnel she'd salvaged from an old dock mech. Inching Cee-Bee across the thin ice fast as she dared, already knowing it was too slow. She couldn't pick up Ruby-Go-Go on visuals, but Cee-Bee's sensors pinged a heat source fifty meters down that was probably Ruby's engines.

The thunder of mechanized footprints told her the race had picked up speed, all their competitors pulling ahead and heading for the finish line.

Maya whispered a silent apology to her mom and inched her way across the ice, spreading Cee-Bee's weight to avoid falling through herself. She readied the grapnel and tried to lock onto the heat source, calculating the trajectories and probably drift thanks to the currents below. "Lex, if you can hear me, I'm dropping a line. I'll get it close to you as I can, but the surface ice is weak here. You'll need to hook yourself so I can haul you back to the surface."

The only response was a squall of radio static, and Maya hoped that meant Alex had picked up something. She lowered the cable and slowly inched back, retreating to the stability of the track. The unspooling cable hung slack, then caught, throwing up shards of ice as the line went taught. The radio squalled a second time, good enough. Maya dug her spikes into the ice and began hauling Ruby-Go-Go to the surface. Cee-Bee's engines fired hard, running hot and throwing up warnings that the shoulder joints were experiencing undue pressure. The synaptic feed through the trodes ensured Dana felt the burn, her own shoulders protesting at the effort.

A second alarm joined the cacophony, Cee-Bee's right knee exceeding safe perimeters and threatening to tear. "Don't you dare," Dana snarled, jamming her feet against the pedals as she sought to shift her weight. "Don't you fucking dare."

The alarm grew shrill, flashing urgent warnings across the console. The right knee wouldn't hold. Dana swore and dropped Cee-Bee's center of gravity, putting mech down on the bad knee. It gave her less traction, with only the left foot driving pitons into the ice, and hauling on the chain twisted Cee-Bee's whole chassis the wrong way, adding new strain to the systems.

Sparks flew across the cockpit, and the squeal of metal straining against metal obliterated Dana's scream.

She hauled and prayed and refused to give up, and caught sight of Ruby-Go-Go's scarlet plating slowly rising to the surface.

"Alex, you've gotta climb," Dana said, unsure if her voice would carry over the racket of Cee-Bee tearing himself apart. Unsure if the radio was even working, with Ruby below the water. "If you've got any power left, you've gotta climb up the goddamn chain."

No answer, not even the static hiss and click. Nothing but the scream of the dying mech as Cee-Bee tried to haul Ruby-Go-Go up, every part of the clunker protesting the effort.

Maya sensed the moment the right knee sheared loose a moment before it happened. The protesting metal tore and she pulled the trodes free, shielding her face as Cee-Bee spun and tumbled across the icy surface. Her gimbaled couch crashed against its limits, jerking her head this way and that. Conscious thought gave way to instinct, one hand carving a furrow into the ice to halt the slide towards the water. Left leg kicking against the snow, traction spikes digging a groove. Cee-Bee was toast—that much as a forgone conclusion—but she could hold the line long enough to get Ruby-Go-Go to the surface, and maybe scramble free of Cee-Bee's cockpit before the big mech went under too.

Please. Dana wasn't much for prayer, wasn't sure who could get out here to help. *Fucking please, give me this one.*

Cee-Bee's reactors redlined with the effort, and her console flashed a warning as every joint shot past its load limits. Dana hauled, twisting with the effort, and hit the eject button on her dash. Cee-Bee's chest chasing sprang free, pressurized mechanisms jettisoning the extraneous part over the water. Frigid air blew in through the opening as the crash couch released Dana, pushing her forward, up and out of the cockpit. Cee-Bee slid across the ice, following the tug of the cable line. Dana scrambled back, heading for the shoulders. She launched herself off, already twisting, preparing to roll with the impact.

Even prepared, the breath wuffed out of her, the sudden impact and dreadful cold merging into a solid punch that stole everything but instinct away. Dana rolled free as Cee-Bee lurched towards the water, grasping fingers tearing up chips of ice as the big mech obeyed her last command, trying to hold on. One arm reaching back, seeking purchase in the ice, one hand stretching toward the water in the faint hope Ruby-Go-Go made up.

The cold set in immediately, cutting through Dana's warm jacket. The adrenaline surge of hope and panic gave way to the pain of her jump, the fear that it had all been for naught, the sheer panic of seeing Cee-Bee slipping towards the edge.

Dana offered a last, pleading thought as the darkness rushed towards her, vision tunneling into the terrible sight of the mech and the cable line. *Please,* she thought, a futile gesture. *Please, just climb.*

It was all she had left, and she was sure it wouldn't be enough.

Dana came to in a warm infirmary bed, tucked beneath a silver thermal blanket keeping her body-heat close. She blinked into the musty light and worked her jaw, then her fingers and toes. Testing everything was still intact, rather than losing bits and limbs to frostbite. The bitter cold of being exposed on the ice still clung to her bones despite the blanket, but her head burned and fought against the fog, trying to piece together what had occurred.

"She's alive." Riordan O'Day's bitter voice caught Dana off-guard, the rasp of it barging against her thoughts from a point to her right. She twisted, body protesting the movement, and found him perched on the small visitor's chair, a hand terminal on his lap. "Medics informed me you were likely to come around this morning, and I thought you should know your intervention saved Alexander's life. Your mech—"

"Cee-Bee," Dana said, a pang of sorrow spearing through her.

"Cee-Bee." The distaste showed on O'Day's face. "Your... Cee-Bee... hauled her up, kept her close enough to the surface for a rescue shuttle to retriever her and get her warm. Frostbitten, but Alexander is still in one piece, and early signs suggest a full recovery. It will delay her academy entry a few months, but it could have been much worse."

"But she's okay?"

"She is."

"Am I?"

O'Day's features hardened at the question, and he pushed himself free of the chair. "My people recovered Alexander's mech and performed a diagnostic. Standard procedure on an accident of this caliber—we can't afford to have the family falling prey to any filatures or malfunctions that could risk their lives. It turns out, someone planted a virus in the mech's systems. Nasty, complex work that could have triggered a systems failure and cost Alexander the race."

He didn't bother with accusation, and Dana didn't have the energy to school her features and play innocent on the matter. "Cee-Bee?"

"I retrieved what I could, as a courtesy. I'm not sure I should have bothered."

"The virus was dormant," Dana said.

O'Day's face went taut, like a knot pulled to breaking point, then relaxed as the anger passed. "My techs confirmed as much when they investigated the cause," he said. "It's the only reason you woke up here, instead of facing charges. I reserve the right to change my mind about that. If any evidence arises that your work caused the accident..."

He let the thread hang, but Dana didn't have the energy to rise to the bait. If she'd caused the accident, whether inadvertently or otherwise, he wouldn't need to press charges. She'd confess and surrender herself to the authorities, let them do whatever the hell they wanted to punish her for the mistake.

"I needed the credits," she said. "My father did something stupid, and it was the only way to get things back on track. But I couldn't do that to Alex."

"It's that simple?"

"She's my friend," Dana said. "I don't have enough of those to waste."

"Perhaps that will still be true once she's recovered enough to hear the details of the story."

"Wait—" Dana surged upright and immediately regretted the decision. Her head swam, and she fell back into the cot, struggling to focus, struggling to think. A monitor to her left beeped, summoning the medic. Riordan O'Day stepped close, looming over her, his expression filled with pity. "I rather wish you'd taken me up on my offer, Miss Halpern. It would have been cleaner than all this."

The fuck-you retort died on Dana's lips. She didn't have the energy to fight anymore, wasn't entirely sure he was wrong. O'Day turned away and strode out of the infirmary, heading down the hall. Dana sank back into the warmth of the blanket, tears prickling the corners of her eyes, as the medic hustled in to check on her.

Three weeks later, fresh out of the infirmary, Maya ventured out into the cold. She sloughed down the snow-thick streets to the pawnshop, pressed her face against the frost-rimmed window. The clutter of Halcyon's store was just as chaotic as it had been a few days before, but the space on the wall where her mother's Strat once hung ate at her. She'd saved Alex, but nothing changed: Alex was still due to ship out to the academy, her grandfather wanted their friendship over, and Maya would be on Javal all alone. Scraping by doing patches on failing mechs, dealing with her father's obsession with changing the world, and trying not to ache every time she thought about the empty spaces her mother once occupied.

Tears brimmed, and Maya blinked them away. Nothing good came from weeping in temperature this cold, and she didn't deserve to be crying. Maya had fucked up, big time. Maya had put recovering the fucking Stratocaster over her best friend in the world. She drew a deep, shuddering breath and steeled herself, stuffing the pain down deep. Maybe she'd get lucky and it'd ferment, turn into anger again. Turn into the kind of anger her mother's punk bands loved to sing about. If being a mechanic was no longer a way off this rock, she'd have to turn to something else. Punk singer was better than nothing, she figured.

Maya allowed herself a quick, choking laugh of regret. Time to make the best of things. She shoved mittened hands into her pockets and forged her way down the snow-covered street. Alexander's father had contacted Maya when Alex made it home from the infirmary, possibly in defiance of Riordan O'Day's orders to the contrary. An invitation had been delivered for Alex's farewell, one last chance to say goodby, and Maya's list of places she'd much rather be considerable, and thought of simply not showing up had occurred to her several times. She followed the street down to the intersection, took a left and headed for the warm, roomy building that had been the O'Day family home for two generations now.

She heard them well before she made it to the front gate. A riot of raised voices, each infused with anger, all of them male and baritone. Less a party in progress, and more like one of the temperamental rows that sent Alex scurrying to the workshop in search of sanctuary.

Maya stood on the doorstep, not yet ready to ring the bell and wade into the O'Day family drama. Unsure if Alex knew what she'd done yet, and whether it had changed everything. She steeled herself, as she always did, and tried not to think ill of Alex's family. You'd think they could hold it together for one last day, especially given the situation. Alex had almost died. Alex was about to leave forever. Alex—

The snowball hit Maya in the side of the head, a soft thump that jarred her thoughts. She whirled, fingers bunching into fists, ready to lash out… and discovered Maya at the edge of the family home, half-way through loading bags onto sled when she instigated a snowball fight.

Maya's heart caught in her throat, strangled her habitual response to say something mean about the childlike way of greeting her best friend. Instead, she crouched and gathered a handful of snow from the slush around the doorway, carefully avoiding the patches turning brown and ugly from churning feet. "Would have thought you'd had enough fun in the cold," she said, then launched her retaliation. It flew over Alex's head, shattered against the neighbor's wall.

Alex poked her tongue out. Inside, Old Man O'Day's voice bellowed a dire warning and something smashed against the wall. Alex flinched at the impact and lowered her defenses. Turned back to the bags and the cart. Maya gave up any pretense she hadn't heard and went over to help her friend load. "You're looking good for a woman who nearly drowned a few weeks back."

"Smartest person I know thought fast and pulled me out," Alex said. "Could have been much worse."

Another squall of raised voices carried out into the street. Maya scowled at the house. "They sound like they're in fine form today."

Alex shrugged and looked away. "They got some news they weren't happy about," she said. "Everyone's looking for someone to blame."

"Business as usual at the O'Days, then?"

"Kind of." Alex offered a weak smile, but it didn't reach her eyes. "Listen, about the race—"

"Yeah," Maya said. "I couldn't leave your ass to freeze to death at the bottom of the bay."

"But you planted a virus to ensure you won and walked away with the prize money?"

Maya opened her mouth to respond, but there wasn't anything there. She met Alex's pale blue eyes and fumbled every excuse that came to mind, working her way through all of them before she settled on the truth. "Your grandfather told you."

"He did."

"I'm sorry." Maya backed away from Alex, from the sled and the bags and the cutting pain of the betrayal. "I went a little nuts, after dad sold the guitar, and I put something in place because I knew... shit, I knew you were better than me. I knew you were going to win. But once we got there, I couldn't… shit. I'm sorry. I couldn't—"

"Hey." Alex closed the distance between them, wrapped Maya in a hug. "It's cool. I know what that axe meant to you, and what it means to have a family who isn't all that."

"I'm sorry," Maya said, and this time tears brimmed and fell. "I still miss her, and you were leaving, and I—"

"Chill, weirdo," Alex said. "It's a billion degrees below right now. Save your tears until we're some place warm."

Maya smiled despite herself, but it still took several sniffs and wipes before she reined her emotions in. Alex waited, smiling to herself, ignoring the squall of argument inside the family home.

Finally, she said: "Can I crash at the workshop tonight?"

The relief that warmed through Maya caught her by surprise. "Long as you want," she said. "Right up until you leave, if that's what you want."

"Could be awhile longer than that," Alex said. "There's been a slight change of plans, on account of the accident. Flight school's delayed until the next rotation."

"What? Come on, you said you were fine—"

"It's not about being hurt," Alex said. "After everything that happened, I just realized this wasn't my rotation. I've got stuff I need to take care of here."

Maya's heart flip-flopped inside her chest, dizzy as a snowflake caught in an updraft and just as likely to disappear if things didn't go right. She tried not to let it show on her face. "Yeah, like what?"

"Like winning a sixth ice run, for starters, and doing it on my terms. I'm thinking you and I should rebuild Cee-Bee, show these assholes what true talent really looks like. Maybe cram it down my grandfather's throat before I fly out."

"Alex, come on. That's—"

"Hey, I got something for you. A little thank you for saving my skin" Alex whirled on her heel and reached inside the doorway. Emerged with the battered guitar case, covered in familiar, worn stickers from all the bands Maya heard in childhood. Alex pressed it into Maya's hands, and the familiar weight of it prickled her eyes with tears.

"What?" Maya said. "How?"

"I already had the credits to get off planet." Alex shoved both hands into her jacket pocket, studying the skyline as she spoke. "More than enough to get it out of hock and get by for a stretch. Seemed like the thank you my grandpa *should* have offered, if he wasn't an unmitigated ass."

"But the academy—"

"Will still be there in a season," Alex said. "And I'd rather go with you than without you, you know? Me and you, we're a team, May. Only reason I agreed to race Ruby this season was to get the money to take you with me when it was time to leave, and I knew you weren't going nowhere without your mom's Strat."

Maya knelt in the snow and peeled off a mitten. She unclipped the case and flipped it open, stared at the cherry red curves and worn frets nestled in the plush cushions that kept the instrument safe. Her mum's signature in the bottom, right next to Maya's crude 8-year-old's hand. She closed up, scarcely daring to breathe, unwilling to expose the Strat to the cold anymore than she needed to.

"Thank you," she said. "You don't know—"

"Bullshit. I know *exactly* what it means to you," Alex said. "Probably better than anyone, including your old man. So how about we skip the crying and finish loading all my stuff—we're going to need a new race mech for next season. Shouldn't need more than one or two wins for a couple of bright young things like us to earn the credits for two tickets off-world, don't you think?"

Maya tucked the guitar case in the corner of Alex's sled, then went to grab the last few bags sitting by the door. Everything Alex owned was right there, crammed into duffles and shipping boxes, ready for transport off planet. Now it was coming to live in the dirty corner of the workshop, living in the shadow of the beat-up mech that wasn't a shadow on Ruby-Go-Go, waiting for a time when they could leave the planet together. Maya pushed everything aboard while Alex strapped the boxes down, ready for transport. She watched the long, powerful arms at work and the smile Alex tried to hide.

"Lex," Maya said, "you know you're my best friend, right?"

"Always stating the obvious." Alex shook her head in mock resignation, but there was no hiding the smile anymore. "You are going to come when I bail on this place, yeah? Academy needs mechanics as well as pilots, and I'm thinking starships are way more exciting than rebuilding mechs out of parts."

"You think they'd accept me?"

"They'd be stupid not to." Alex grabbed Maya by the arm and pulled her into a hug. "If the idea holds some appeal to you."

Maya chewed it over.

It wasn't a hard decision at all.

STORY NOTES

THE CARS

I grew up in an era where car headlights were round or oddly square, depending on the vehicles age. Then the design aesthetic changing my early teens, with the introductions of sleeker, eye-shaped headlights as standard.

I was just young enough to start daydreaming about cars as predatory creatures, and after twenty years of percolation his story emerged.

It's helped, I suspect, by the slow emergence of self-driving vehicles as a reality rather than a science fictional conceit, to say nothing of COVID teaching all of us what it's like when everyday things disappear.

PUT NOT YOUR FAITH IN HOPE

Optophobia is a fear of opening one's eyes, and a writing prompt that came my way. Prompts always lend themselves to obvious approaches, and writing a story about a character who can't open their eyes felt like a well-trade approach. Instead, I wrote about an entire city trapped in a god's eye, simultaneously curious and terrified about what might happen when the god's eyelid rose after centuries.

I suspect I'll return tot he city go God's Eye for a future story. Much as I like this short piece, I feel like there's far more to be done with the concept.

FOUR MOHOCKS, SENT ABROAD

The Mohocks were a real eighteenth century gang in London, but I first learned of them courtesy of *Brewers Dictionary of Phrase and Fable*. They've always struck me as semi-mythical as a result.

This was one of the first stories I write and liked after a long spell away from writing, putting all my focus on publishing other people through Brain Jar Press. My whole goal was to write something fun and get lost in the narrator's voice.

MEDIAN SURVIVAL TIME

This began as a homage to Ernest Hemingway's *Hills Like White Elephants*, which features two characters talking around a topic without ever addressing it directly. Over the years I've given lectures on the technique and craft of the story, and just how hard said techniques are to replicate. Hemingway's refusal to give us access to either character's interiority, essentially treating them as actors on a stage rather than deploying a close point of view, leaves the reader to rely on subtext to figure out what's going on.

We spend considerably more time in Eleanor Holst's perspective here than either of Hemingway's characters, but even so, it felt like an interesting departure from my normal habits as a writer. I started a longer book about Holst and the aftermath of this story, but found it hard to write that kind of slow, coiling menace during the lockdown of 2020.

One day soon, I should unearth that draft and see whether it might be completed…

WARM MILK & WHISKEY

This story emerged from a genre mash-up writing prompt, asking authors to blend film noir with farce. In my head, that terrain is already taken by Alan Parker's 1976 musical film *Bugsy Malone,* where pre-teen gangsters wage war with guns that fire whipped cream. It was one of the few films I saw multiple times as a young kid, courtesy of friends who had it on VCR. It's been thirty years since I last saw it, but parts of the film remain permanently lodged in my head.

The only logical thing that would make the concept more farcical was to make the characters even younger.

THE FUCKING-SHITFULL-GODDAMNED-ASSHOLE-NOODLECOCKED-MOTHERFUCKER HAS TO DIE

This started with a writing prompt about using excessive amounts of profanity, and wound its way to one of my favorite tactics of contrasting seemingly mundane, pragmatic heroes against the folderol and drama of the supernatural.

THIS IS HOW YOU STEP UP

Like many children of 80s science fiction, I possess an affection of the sub-genre of post-apocalyptic fiction where brave heroes drive fast cars across sun-blasted wastelands. When I was challenged to write a story about a car chase, this was the inevitable result.

I wrote a large chunk of this on my morning commute to work during the second covid wave, feeling very conflicted about the idea of being out in the world and the relentless workload I found waiting for me once I made it to the office. The idea of stepping up was very much wish fulfillment. Hell, even dealing with carnivorous road gangs and cyborg dinosaurs struck me as a better class of problems than anything I'd face at work.

THE FIGHTER

I wrote this as a little palate cleanser while drafting the first Dana Valkyrie novella, which meant I had underground MMA fight and science fiction on the brain. Dana's stories tend to be reeling, let-me-impress-you-with-this-tale-of-woe narratives, and I wanted to write something more hardboiled.

It was also a story inspired by countless fighting games which emerged after the success of the Street Fighter franchise, finding a way to succinctly give the impression of a tournament filled with wild characters and interrupted by cut scenes.

IT'S NOT A JOB

This was an attempt to poke fun at the "chosen one" narrative which so often appears in fantasy and its various sub-genres, especially on television. The struggle against one's destiny is a frequent subplot in many of these tales, particularly in urban fantasy, and I wanted to write a hero who actually got the chance to walk away rather than feeing beholden to destiny.

NOS, THE BEETLE SLAYER

I was a RPG gamer before I was a writer, and while gaming tropes often infect my stories, it's rare I take characters I've played or words I've run games in and use them as a foundation for fiction.

This is one of those rare exceptions to the rule. Nos started life as the short, yappy sidekick to an escaped gladiator in a friend's Call o C'Thulhu-inspired fantasy setting. I envisioned him as the anti-Conan: short, boastful, and vaguely competent, but far better at stabbing people in the back than defeating them in a fair fight.

INFECTION VECTORS

A story set in Helix City, a cyberpunk vision of Brisbane which appears in my stories *Deadbeats* and *Clockwork, Patchwork, and Ravens*, along with some forthcoming novel projects. Usually, I start these stories by combing cyberpunk tropes with fairytale motifs and twisting both until they seem to fit. Infection Vectors took a slightly different tack, although I'm still fond of the results.

ON THE CORNER OF CAXTON AND PETRIE, 12:04 AM

I am old and tired and do not enjoy going to night clubs and bars anymore, so on the rare occasion I find myself in such situations I'm usually daydreaming about distractions which might allow me to escape.

Usually, I daydream about the zombie apocalypse breaking out, but time-traveling viking raiders strike me as an equally useful excuse for calling it a night.

A GOOD THIEF'S CHOICES

I still think of myself as a Dungeons and Dragons player, but in truth it's been fifteen years since I last played a fantasy RPG, having long-since drifted towards playing horror games and running superhero campaigns.

While I doubt I'll ever have the chance to run a fully-fledged, 1st level to 20th level campaign again, I dearly want to run an ongoing campaign using John Harper's incredible *Blades In The Dark* game about fantasy heists and thievery.

Even then, my attempts to get a game off the ground were thwarted by the 2020 lockdowns, so I occasionally settle for writing short stories about fantasy thieves instead.

THE CHAP WHO WANTED TO BE COMMANDER FLAGG

I wrote this a few years back as a birthday present for my friend Allan, who is often better known as the prop-maker and brains behind Type 40 Productions. The two of us have been building creative careers on very similar timeframes, albeit in very different fields, and we've spent a good chunk of the last decade or two catching up and talking about business.

Three things about Allan that's worth knowing here:

1. When not making inventive pop-culture props for cosplayers, he runs one of the finest Call of Cthulhu roleplaying campaigns one might ever hope to play in.
2. He's an Englishman living in Australia, and the kind of affably charming chap who'll befriend people everywhere.
3. He has an astonishingly good Steve Rodgers cosplay, which is a whole mess of cognitive dissonance when combined with his location and accent.

Naturally, when I set out to write him a story, I set it against the backdrop of alien invaders and Cosplayers stepping up to save the world.

ONE LAST JOB, THEN SLEEP

I wrote a huge chunk of this story while listening to Deerhoof's song *Panda Panda Panda,* three minutes of lurching noise-punk with some of the most inane lyrics you'll ever hear. The whole song is a terrifying ear worm, and this story was an attempt to exorcise it.

Which tells you absolutely nothing about the story's contents, but does explain why the name Dickerhoof left me grinning.

THE DEAL

I was doing a workshop for a bunch of teenage writers tasked with producing a short crime story after reading a series of novels, and we were talking about using the weight of the genre against itself when you're working to a strict word count.

I wrote the first two hundred words of this story as an exercise during the workshop, and I don't like to let such things go to waste. I figured it would come out as a crime story in the end, but I'm a speculative fiction writer at heart and it wasn't long before there were demons appearing and dangerous bargains to be made.

I'M AFRAID OF THE BIG BAD WOLF

I don't believe in ghosts or werewolves or supernatural phenomena, but this story has more basis in reality than most of my fiction.

The Gold Coast, where I grew up, is a very strange place and I would be totally unsurprised to learn werewolves lived in the hills despite my firm belief werewolves don't exist.

OR FOR ETERNITY HOLD YOUR PEACE

I often tell writers I'm mentoring to look for rituals in their characters lives, because disrupting a ritual so it doesn't go to plan is an easy way to tell the reader shit has hit the fan for the characters. Occasionally this leads to the most cliched of interrupted rituals, one which only seems to happen in stories: answering when a priest asks if there is any reason two people should not marry.

I've seen it hundreds of times in romance stories, so I challenged myself to a version which leant towards horror instead.

SIX CATS GO CAMPING

I didn't grow up with pets, but I moved in with a girlfriend who owned two in my early thirties and suddenly understood why every speculative fiction writers seems to mention theirs in their bio. I wrote a very fast-and-loose version of this story as a present for said girlfriend many years ago, then set it aside after we broke up and I no longer lived with cats.

When I moved in with my wife, over a decade later, we ended up adopting a cat named Admiral Coco Marshmallow Flerkin-Wittingstall. For the first time ever I had a pet I'd chosen to have, and The Admiral promptly took over my social media feed as I fell in love with cats all over agin. Not long after I found myself digging around in my drafts folder to revisit this story and produce a longer version.

I also love the conceit of stories within stories, and I really want to write a few more of these stories to find out what tales the other cats were planning on telling before the night was cut short.

THE FINAL SEASON

A few years ago I made a joke about merging *The Fast and The Furious: Tokyo Drift* and *Pacific Rim* in a room of fellow writers. Someone wondered what that would look like, so I started putting elements in place: bored kids in a futuristic Alaska; stealing giant mecha to race across sheets of ice, ending in a skid roughly equivalent to sliding across polished wooden floors in socks.

The final story took a whole bunch of turns and changes, and it took me nearly eight years to finish a draft, but what started as a joke idea felt more and more serious by the time I'd finished.

ACKNOWLEDGMENTS

This book wouldn't exist without Patreon.

Publishing commentator Craig Mod once dubbed patronage and similar mentorship programs "implicit and durable permission machines"*, de-coupling the creative process from the demands of the broader market and allowing artists to take chances they wouldn't otherwise take.

For three years, I wrote stories for the Eclectic Projects supporters without thinking about where I would send the finished work or which editors tastes they might fit. It changed the way I wrote, for good or for ill, and resulted in many stories I wouldn't have finished otherwise.

While the Eclectic Projects Patreon no longer runs, my sincere thanks go out to the folks who threw their financial and emotional support behind this project over the years: Margaret Ball, Kate Eltham, Nicole Strickland, Jodi, Meg Vann, Sally Ball, Jennifer White, Maggie Slater, David Versace, Mark Webb, Seagoat, Kathleen Jennings, Kylie Scott, Tansy Rayner Roberts, Lois Spangler, Ben Francisco, Anja Peerdeman, Trent Jamieson, Catherine Caine, and Stephanie Gunn. You all rock.

Special thanks also go out to my spouse-mouse, Sarah "Zazz" Hobday, who puts up with a good deal of weirdness and occasionally has to remind me there is life outside the stories I'm conjuring in my head. You are awesome and I love you.

Finally, writers tend to accumulate a crew of friends and allies who are a source of great advice, challenging conversation, and vocal support that keeps things moving forward. My thanks

---

* In the essay *Running a Successful Membership / Subscription Program*, available on his website here: https://craigmod.com/essays/successful_memberships/

go out to Team Write Club—Angela Slatter, Kathleen Jennings, and Joanne Anderton—and the Sunday Night Cthulhu Crew of Allan Carey, Nicola Logan, Nic Holland, and Adam Norris.

ABOUT THE AUTHOR

PETER M. BALL is an author, publisher, and RPG gamer whose love of speculative fiction emerged after exposure to *The Hobbit*, *Star Wars*, David Lynch's *Dune*, and far too many games of *Dungeons and Dragons* before the age of 7. He's spent the bulk of his life working as a creative writing tutor, with brief stints as a performance poet, gaming convention organiser, online content developer, non-profit arts manager, and d20 RPG publisher.

Peter's three biggest passions are fiction, gaming, and honing the way aspiring writers think about the business and craft of writing, which led to a five-year period working for Queensland Writers Centre as manager of the Australian Writers Marketplace and convenor of the GenreCon writing conference. He has a PhD in creative writing, specialising in series poetics and digital publishing.

Peter is the brain-in-charge at Brain Jar Press, delivers regular advice for writers at GenrePunk.Ninja, and publishes his own work under the GenrePunk Books imprint. Peter can be found online at: www.petermball.com

facebook.com/Petermball

instagram.com/petermball

threads.net/@petermball

goodreads.com/petermball

THANK YOU FOR BUYING THIS GENREPUNK BOOKS COLLECTION

To receive special offers, bonus content, and info on new releases and other great reads, sign up for Peter M. Ball's weekly newsletter at www.petermball.com/newsletter.

www.ingramcontent.com/pod-product-compliance
Lightning Source LLC
Chambersburg PA
CBHW011559190726

48287CB00010B/2965